C000093220

DON`T LAUGH AT ME,
I'M JUST THE DRIVER

To The Credit Card Queen

Enjoy

Steven Evans

Love

S.T. Evans

12-5-11

authorHOUSE®

AuthorHouse™ UK Ltd.
500 Avebury Boulevard
Central Milton Keynes, MK9 2BE
www.authorhouse.co.uk
Phone: 08001974150

©2011. Steven Evans. All rights reserved

No part of this book may be reproduced, stored in a retrieval system, or transmitted by any means without the written permission of the author.

First published by AuthorHouse   04/16/2011

ISBN: 978-1-4567-7639-8 (sc)

Any people depicted in stock imagery provided by Thinkstock are models, and such images are being used for illustrative purposes only. Certain stock imagery © Thinkstock.

This book is printed on acid-free paper.

Because of the dynamic nature of the Internet, any web addresses or links contained in this book may have changed since publication and may no longer be valid. The views expressed in this work are solely those of the author and do not necessarily reflect the views of the publisher, and the publisher hereby disclaims any responsibility for them.

Introduction

Where do you start when you write a book? It's easy to say from the beginning but where's the beginning? My beginning started when I was in my 20`s and in three months time I'll be 41. I've read this book and I question myself. Did all this really happen? Did I really do these things? I'm a different person now, or am I?

Today when I saw Renaud I said to him, "I'm going to get my ISBN number today".
His reaction was "Good, it's been going on for four years". It's true; it's been four years since I decided people would find my story interesting. The title, 'Don't Laugh At Me, I'm Just The Driver' came from a friend Gerald. I rang him up and set him the challenge and as usual, within hours he'd come up with one. I told him I wanted a story connection but not too direct and that it needed to sound funny. He came up with the above. I worried at the beginning that it was too long but then I got used to it. My first title was going to be `The Ups And Downs Of A Limo Driver's Knickers` but out of respect for SNW I changed it. Thanks Darran for the original and thanks Gerald for the new title.

I was in Spain when I first wrote the book, sitting outside every day in the sunshine on a bench, writing and writing and writing. 'Hola' was my only conversation, I couldn't speak Spanish, I think the locals thought I was a bit of a loopy English man. In a way I was. I met some nice people in Spain, Daniel is a good friend, Kevin `Katie Peters` is my favourite. He did drag in some of the local bars and to date he's one of the funniest men I've met. Daniel took over my barbers shop `Mr Grimsdales`, there's your clue. My first draft was sent to some friends, R&R, they lost it. The second draft I kept and when I came back to the UK I found it wasn't in my boxes. The one box which went missing and my book was in it.

You'll probably laugh all through the book, I wrote it with you in mind. I have virtually skipped the first 16 years, nothing much happened and having read loads of biographies, I find the early years are quite drawn out. I'm currently reading the autobiography of Ozzy Osbourne, I recently met him and got him to sign my book. The book is so funny, I hope you find mine the same.

I want to thank a few people, Renaud for not losing patience, my Mum Sylvia and Pete for their everlasting support, my Dad Derek for the advice, memories and history and my brothers Jason and David. Thanks to Aunty Sue & Mick and Aunty June & Kat for their stories and photos. Also thanks to Norman for making me who I am and to K and N for allowing him. Huge thanks to LC for years of support and Gerald for the title again. Initials are to protect the innocent or their privacy; I didn't realize how protective people are over using their names. Thanks to Delphine for the cover and Daniel for his words.

I want to dedicate this book to my children Daniel and Jason, "Boys, I hope this book gives you the inspiration to find yourselves. It's time to grow up and be lucky. Don't miss out, as this world is spinning around you 24/7. I love you both."

Thank you for buying my book, enjoy it for what it is, my story. Enjoy.

The boy who wanted more.., As I child I spent a lot of my time watching TV, the `Carry On` films, Are you being served, Benny Hill and Norman Wisdom films, little did I know that my life would take a turn and I'd be working with some of my favourite actors, indeed become friends with them.

As I sat on the floor I looked at the man to my right, he was asleep in his chair. I held his hand, his breathing was quiet and his lips old and dry. The hand was old and wrinkled; I stroke the skin on the back of his hand "this hand has shaken the hands of Royalty, Stars, Singers and Actors. The hand has performed over 70 years on stage, film, TV and here I am holding it. The skin was pale, slight bruising and purple patches of colour "Sorry Steve, did I nod off" came the voice of this old man, his eyes looked tired and sad but his smile was beaming "don't worry Norman" I said "I'm used to you dropping off" he gave a little chuckle, a familiar laugh.

Norman Wisdom is my mate, he changed my life and i want everyone to know this,

Thanks Jo for helping me re write my book, your help was unconditional and I'm proud of you.

I was born on the 22nd March 1969, yeah I'm 40...I know! I can't believe it myself. I was born in Aldershot within the camp walls, my father was a Coldstream Guard apparently. I didn't know this until I was 17 but you can read that bit when you get to it. I was discussing this with my dad recently. "How far back can you remember?" I asked. I didn't believe people when they said they could remember when they were two years old but guess what, my earliest memory is of the Aldham housing estate in Wombwell nr Barnsley. When I asked my mum how old I must have been, she said "About two years old", so there you go. We had an apartment there, we knew it as a flat, ground floor with a white leather settee. My memory is of daddy long legs flying around every where. "Err get off you little bastards", oops sorry, I still freak out.

From there we went to Hawson St, Wombwell. This was a nice big house at the bottom of a street; nr the canal, 5p electricity meter, garden all round, it was the bee's knees. The truth is it was damp, smelly and haunted but I liked it. When we moved in, the previous owners had left a locked tool shed so I helped my dad break the lock and it was a treasure trove of shit. It was great rummaging through the boxes, there were old radios, tools, clocks, nails and screws, jars and jars of screws. I loved finding this treasure and playing with the broken radios. At Hawson St we worked out I was allergic to cats or should I say, cat's wee. I fell face first into some cat piss and my face was swollen like the Elephant man's face. I couldn't see for days because my cheeks had covered my eyes. Needless to say I have avoided cats since.

1

Jason my younger brother must have been born around about this time because David my older brother had decided to take Jason out to the canal. I remember a panic stricken mum when she realised Jason was missing and worse still, David was with him. My Mum grabbed hold of my arm and we ran to the canal. After only a few minutes David was spotted on an embankment trying to convince Jason to cross the 12ft drop on a thick black pipe bridging the water. David has always been the daredevil; I'd seen him swinging off this pipe with his mates. Mum was furious, she dropped her lager and ran up to him screaming "You little bleeder, wait 'til I tell your Dad". Elvis must have died when we lived here because I remember the neighbours, inc my Mum screaming and wailing in the streets, well maybe not wailing but to me it sounded this way.

There must have been some interest in girls on Hawson St. One night it had gotten dark early and heavy rain had started to fall. Knowing me I would have been bored and I decided to see if this girl was at home, a neighbour. I knocked on the door, there was no answer so I walked around to the back. There was a faint light so I pressed my nose up against the window, just as the girl was getting out of a tin bath. She looked directly at me and when she saw me she screamed the fucking street down. I ran home, said hi to my parents and went upstairs out of the way. A good 5 minutes later I'd calmed down and decided to venture downstairs where Mum and Dad were talking quite seriously. That night, we kids got a warning from my parents. "There's been a pervert hanging around the streets, don't talk to any strangers. Are you listening to me?" my Mum said. I was listening but I was more scared of them finding out it was just me.

From there we moved to some real neighbours, a real street and a real council estate. It was a 2 up 2 down, it was great; 68 St Helens Ave, Smithies, Barnsley. I can't think why but I felt quite posh at this house, I felt like we'd made it even though my Mum was working in a bookies and my poor Dad was a Binman. My Mum has always worked hard but I felt sorry for my Dad, he must have been knackered carrying these bins in and out the gardens. It certainly kept him fit, he'd often stand in front of a mirror and say "I'm in my prime", and he was. I started school at Athersley Infant School, moving on to St Helens comprehensive. I hated school, everything about it, the regime, the meals, the staff and the subjects. It's only now I realise how I actually had a good time there. I quite enjoyed it but back then it was hell, with the school bells and the slop they called food.

Mr Davies (A) was my form teacher. God knows what he thought about me but he never hit me or shouted at me, I think he tolerated me or found my constant lies amusing. I often 'wagged' school, which is `Barnsley` for playing truant. I'd walk the streets, camp out, even work on the market. My favourite was looking around showrooms for caravans, trailers and tents. I loved it and found it a means of escape and privacy. Poor Mr Davies always spotted my fake notes from my Mum, normally it was explaining why I'd not been in to school for three weeks. `Mr Davies, Steven has not been to school because he has chopped his head off, regards blah blah blah`. His words or tone will never leave me.

"Another handwriting Steve, you must think I'm barmy", inevitably I'd end up getting a bollocking from the head `Dr Snuggles`. Well, Mr Hesketh actually but everyone called him Dr Snuggles. Whilst I was at the school, the poor man got killed in a car accident. The film `KES` was filmed at our school and one of the characters was our very own Dr Snuggles, he was a teacher playing a teacher. The disappointment was shocking when I was told a year before I started at St Helens there was a teacher who had got the sack for messing with kids. I've always felt left out, no buggers ever tried to get hold of me.

I had a few friends at school, Darren Sedgewick and Andrew Webber. My mates on the street were Andrew, Neil, Shane, Mark, Robert and their families, some I still see when I visit. We had two women living next door, Bridgette and Sharon. They were great fun, they had the cheek of the devil and I loved it. We had an Asian family living in the street, Gabriel was a good mate of my brothers and we also had a family living down the road who were from Belgium. Next door to them were the Cook family. I got on well with both mother and son although Dave used to skin rabbits in front of me which wasn't endearing. Down the street lived my grandparents, Nellie and Fred, I'll tell you their stories in a while. My Mum's parents lived over in Wombwell. I think it's fair to say we didn't see much of them compared to my Dad's but we did see them often. My Granddad was called Tom and Grandmother Irene. Whilst at St Helens Ave, my Mum's mum died suddenly (1973), it was a shock to everyone but my Mum was completely devastated, she still is really. "I never had her long enough" my mum would say, I agreed, we didn't. The night she died my grandparents were approaching their Ruby Anniversary and the family had been planning a surprise holiday for them. My grandmother woke my granddad to ask him to open a watch she'd bought him for their anniversary. She then asked him to make a cuppa and whilst he was gone she passed away, bless her. My granddad never got over her death, neither did the children. She wasn't old, she was approaching retirement and looking forward to more time with the family. I always remember my Gran having a photo in her cabinet of a man showing off his Victoria Cross. He had won the VC for piloting mini submarines in the war; his name was James Magennis, 1919 to 1986. There's a mural of him apparently in Belfast. My mum knew him as Jim and I'm currently searching his history.

My Dad's parents were approx the same age as my Mum's. They moved from a place called Wilthorpe to a bungalow in Athersley. My dad tells a story about my Gran cooking in the house in Wilthorpe, the kids in the lounge and granddad in bed. Bless her, my Gran wasn't good with sausages and one day she set fire to the curtains, running through the house screaming and gathering up the kids.
"Come on, come on, get out there's a fire, call 999, get the fire truck out!" she screamed.
They were out in the streets with all the neighbours when my dad said `Hey Mum, where's my Dad?'
My Gran said "He's in bed, leave him he'll be fine". He was fine.
My Gran used to scare the shit out of me, she used to read tea leaves and palms and talk to herself. In the Poltergeist movies there's a little plump lady, and my Gran was the spitting image of her. Granddad Fred came into his own later into his 70`s. To me, my Gran was the woman in the house and my Granddad was the worker, he repaired wheels on the trucks used in the mines. He had two half fingers missing, I asked what had happened and he told me a truck had been running at speed and the brakes failed, slicing off his fingers.
"What happened next?" I asked him.

He said "I got £700 compensation, we went to Blackpool for a week but I came back after a day, I couldn't stand it". Typical Yorkshire man, I loved him to bits.

My Granddad Tom used to take us to see the gypsies down in Wombwell Woods, he knew them well and they welcomed him as a friend. I loved it down there, living in a caravan with the open spaces and fresh air must have been great. I always thought they were wonderfully friendly people and lucky to be traveling around. My Gran made the most amazing cakes on Sundays, the table was stuffed with Apple Pie, Victoria Sponge, Bilberry Pie (Mum's favourite), buns, scones and sandwiches. It didn't take me long to work out why we visited on Sundays, with a feast like that we couldn't keep away. Except for the time David was playing in the yard and he decided to jump off the shed roof. We found him screaming and hanging by his wrist. A rusty washing line nail had caught him as he fell and had gone straight through his wrist. He was hanging by it , blood spurting everywhere. He's probably still got the scar.

To me we seemed posh; we had three ponds in the back garden. One large one with a waterfall to the other and a waterfall to the third, along with a sand pit, a patio, patio doors and PVC windows. You're seething with jealousy aren't you, I can tell. All I can say is business must have been good. My parents had just bought a `Bookmakers`, commonly known as a Betting shop. I had a rabbit as a pet at this time, `Zoë`, she was lovely, white and fluffy. Even my parents fell in love with her. They didn't really mind when she would shit everywhere, mostly behind the TV. Obviously they didn't encourage it but for "Zoe" it was hop, skip and shit. I liked her cage clean and tidy, saw dust on the floor, fresh water and food, it was a bloody shock the day I got up and she'd froze to death. Bless her; I didn't put in the straw because it was messy, not tidy. I buried her and my Mum said "She'll be running around the fields with other rabbits in heaven". Years later when my dog died, she said the very same thing. "He'll be running around the fields with other dogs in heaven". Chasing our fucking Zoe I thought, bless him/her.

We used to baby-sit ourselves at this time, David would bugger off to his girlfriend's and I'd be left with Jason and the house. I was always bored and looking to make money. I decided to sell chips for

10p out of the kitchen window and I got away with it for a while, until Mum noticed the spuds were disappearing. One particular night my parents went out with my Aunty Pam and Glen, I was babysitting Jason and Glynn, my cousin. The time was getting on, it had gone midnight and I was starting to worry that something had happened. This was unusual as they were never late. Anyway, within minutes Glen's car pulled up so I went to the back door to unlock it just as the door opened. My Aunty Pam walked in, blood all over her fingers and face, then Glen walked in with not a mark on him. Then came my Dad with bloody hands and face and finally my Mum, covered head to toe in mushy peas. She had the most serious look on her face, something like `You dare say a word`! Now, of course it's my favourite mother story. It transpires this girl was in the queue at the Pie `n` Pea stand not the co-op car park and she was complaining that my Mum and Pam had pushed into the queue. Of course they hadn't but before my Mum could give her a 'Barnsley kiss' (punch), this girl threw her pie and peas head to toe over my Mother. Pam joined in, Dad punched her husband (I think he felt left out) and Glen drove the getaway car. Except they didn't really get away because while my mum was on top of this girl pulling her perm out and my Aunty Pam was punching anyone in sight. This girl screamed she'd lost her ring, her dead grandmother had given it to her. Mum, being a mother, stopped battering her and they all helped to look for the ring, they didn't find it. The boyfriend told my parents she had made it up so they all shook his hand and parted company.

To this day we piss ourselves laughing at this story. I also remember when Mum decided we'd visit my Aunty Pat and Uncle Les. We drove to the house, Mum said "Wait here, I want to surprise her", and she jumped out of the car and flew into the house. Only a second later I said "She's gone into the wrong house". She had, and worse still it took her minutes to come out, very red in the cheeks. Apparently she ran into the house, popped her head round to say hi to Les and ran into the kitchen to find her sister wasn't there, so what does my mum do, she lights a fag. The poor man taking a kip on his own sofa woke to find a strange woman having a fag in his kitchen. Embarrassed, my Mum made her apology and left abruptly. Priceless. My Dad was just as bad. Like when he spent a good six months telling me our Piranha (no name or teeth) could suck the skin off our fingers and then he'd stick his finger in and the bloody thing would try. I could see the advantage.

I was about 15 when I got hold of a pellet gun, I had been mating around with a lad called David and he was good at killing things and skinning them, I wasn't amused as you can imagine. We took this gun into the field looking for some bait; I saw a bird in the trees and took aim. I shot the bird, it fell to the ground, fluttered around a bit and then it stopped and I assumed it was dead. The first thing that went through my head was `Why?' Why the hell did I do that? I couldn't believe I had killed it. When I got home my bragging had caught up with me and my Dad was waiting. "Where's the gun?" he said. I handed it over and got a smacked arse, I deserved it. I never did find out what he'd done with the gun but then I didn't care. I've always been uncomfortable with weapons in the house and I assumed my Dad felt the same way. Sometimes on a weekend or a sunny day we would walk to my Grandparent's house. My Gran always spoilt us, normally with some cake and a bit of cash. Sometimes we would go to their local park and swimming pool. Regretfully we didn't seem to see my Granddad on my Mum's side, yes we used to visit but it was two bus journeys away so it wasn't often. Years later, I did get to know him a little more and we regularly joined him for a drink at his local bar.

School was still around, everyday was a struggle. I honestly thought I was learning nothing and couldn't wait to leave. I started dating a girl `Mich`, she was a dog. No, I'm not taking the piss but she wasn't born with a face like an angel; if she did they must have dropped her halfway. My Mother met her Mum at the bookies, mum said she was a regular. I think they had an impression that we had money and one day I saw her talking to my Mother, "Lend me the money for ten fags and I'll let your Steve go out with Mich". I saw my Mother give her the Money! Working with my Mum at the bookies was great; it was a good size betting office with one big room and our space behind the cash desk. We were protected by a reinforced door and thick metal railings. We didn't really need the protection, not with my Mother. This particular day, this guy had lost about £600 and it was towards the end of the day. He was going to the pub, coming back to make a bet and then going off to the pub again. He was getting a bit stroppy and he walked up to the cashier's desk, he pulled out what to me looked like a small pen knife and threatened my Mum. "You fucking cow, you've taken my money", he said. My Mum was furious and climbed off her stool, unlocked the bloody door, confronted this man and pushed him towards the door. I was behind her and she was screaming, "Don't you threaten me, don't you make threats in front of my son". With that, she pushed him out of the door. I believe he came back in the day after with some flowers to apologise. It's the first time I've witnessed my Dad giving my Mother a real bollocking, "What's the point of having bloody bars if you are going to unlock the door and confront them?" He had a point but my Mum's always been a fighter, straight John Bull.

At this time I was mating around with Vernon and his family. I'd often stay over or he'd stay over at my place. We used to talk a lot about get rich quick schemes, delivering yellow pages or chopping up wood and selling it. Vernon was a bit more bulky than me so he was cool to hang around with, I wasn't picked on. We had some good neighbours, the McDonald family lived a few doors from us, and it was great to have mates close by. It was Christmas and my parents had gone out with Barbara and Ez. I'm not sure what happened but this particular Sunday morning, my Mum had a black eye, Barbara had a broken arm and my Dad and Ez were fine. Apparently my mother had been arguing with Barbara at the front gate and Barbara had taken a swing at my Mum, so my Mum pushed her and she lost her balance falling, over the gate. I tell you, it all went off at St Helens Ave. They were still mates for years to come.

In 1983 my brother bought a Mini, a little orange Austin Mini, I loved it. I used to watch him, drilling, filling, grinding and repairing this little car until it was a lovely shade of undercoat grey. David was working most days so as soon as I had come home from school I'd grab the keys and sit inside it and start the engine, it sounded sweet. It wasn't long before I'd started to reverse it off the drive and back on and then one day, I just took it out and around the block and back again. This one day turned to another and I took it further, onto Carlton hill, and it was a bloody hill. I soon realised why David never took it out, there were no brakes, only a hand brake slightly working.

It was too late, I was halfway down this terrible hill and I couldn't slow down. I quickly got it down to second gear and swung left onto a little side road, my feet pushing down for dear life, eventually she stopped. I never took her out again. My love for cars had taken over me, I loved them all and wanted one but it was to be a few years before I got one.

Work? What about my nails?

I vaguely remember leaving school; it wasn't exciting because my parents were always shouting "Welcome to the real world" and "You're going to have to find a job". Find a job? Why? I'd just left one institution. Before I could breath I was offered a YTS scheme for £27.50 a week, I was repairing and re-upholstering settees! Apart from the staple gun fights it was a shit job but I had my wage to look forward to, £12.50 a week. Mum took £15 for my board which I thought was extortionate but truth be known I got most of it back, a quid here and a quid there. On the YTS I met Susan. She was tall, intelligent and beautiful. We got on really well, we started dating.

My Aunty June had a partner called Selli, they were Country and Western Singers, singing in clubs and pubs around Britain. They were called `Silver Dollar` and they were good, always in demand and they won numerous awards. My Aunty June is a great comedian and the audience would fall about laughing when, in taking the piss out of Selli, she would call her `a mucky fast cat`, or when she'd tell mildly filthy jokes and finish with a cracking impression of Tina Turner. My grandparents never discussed their relationship but June told me that my Gran would often say to her "When are you going to make an honest woman of her?" It was a kind of acknowledgement. The subject was approached once in the local working men's club toilets, my Granddad had gone to the gents and he overheard two men talking. "Them two girls on stage, their lesbians" they said. My Granddad went crazy at them, 'idle gossiping' he called it and he punched the one who was speaking, getting himself a temporary `Barring` from the club. He must have apologised because he was back in the week after. The only nuisance my granddad ever caused was with the bingo. If he shouted, you could hear everyone saying

"Hold on, it's only Fred, it could be wrong" and the majority of the time it was. We never minded, we loved him to bits.

Susan and I had finished our YTS and we were looking for work. My Mum told me about a friend of hers from school, Pam Angel. She was the manageress of CI, Community Industries; they were government run and they paid better than the YTS. I rang up and made an appointment for both of us. I was interviewed by Pam, she was lovely, very friendly and as soon as I mentioned my Mum she said I'd got the job. And once more, Susan was working with me. I ended up working in a graveyard (Thanks Mum), cleaning the grounds, the headstones and re-pointing the church spire, inside and out. I've never seen spiders like I had seen inside that spire. We had to go right to the top with scaffolding and sit on the cross members holding the church bell. One day we were all at the top, cleaning away the pigeon crap, masses of it and feathers everywhere. Just as we were getting ready to come down for lunch, George (THE FOREMAN) said "Shit, we are too late". As he looked down through the small window he saw a funeral party walking up the path. Apparently the Vicar had asked him to get us out of the way for when the funeral party arrived, it was too late. We made small talk to pass the time. We could hear the Vicar doing his best when all of a sudden the bell started up with a `ding dong ding dong`, it was deafening, `Luggie`, a lad with big ears, had dropped his lump hammer which landed on the bell, then it hit the wood and bounced back onto the bell again. George was furious; we had to wait until the end of the ceremony and go down to make our apologies. The Vicar wouldn't hear of it, he said the service went well and when the bell started to ring the widow started to laugh. "That'll be him", she said. "Pissed again". Somewhere at the top of that spire is a plaque with all our names engraved on to it, we had it done before we finished the job.

I had been dating Susan for quite a while, maybe 18 months when she fell pregnant, I never really thought about the possibility. I lost my virginity to her and I think I thought it would take a few years before any real `baby batter` appeared so I didn't worry about it too much. Well it didn't take long at all and she was pregnant. When I told my Mum, my brother David was in the lounge. It was quite late evening, about 10pm when I told her. I planned it this way as I knew she would tell my Dad for me and sweeten it a bit first.

I said to my Mum "I think Susan's pregnant". They both looked at me.

"THINK! THINK! What do you mean think?" My Mum said.

I quickly followed with "Well the truth is she is and we are going to get married".

My brother butted in first with his usual wisdom, "I can understand you supporting your girlfriend but getting married, that's a bit extreme".

I tried to explain that I wanted to do the right thing. My Mum lit a fag; I could see she was thinking 'Hmm new skirt or maybe a dress suit, shoes and a hat'. That was it, end of conversation. I went to bed and waited for my dad to come home from the pub. It was maybe 20 minutes later and I heard him coming upstairs, I thought here we go bollocking time but no! He did his usual thing, got changed, went to the loo and went back downstairs. I could hear Mum talking to him, David had stayed up to hear the drama but there wasn't any. The next morning I went downstairs and my Dad was in the kitchen, at first it felt a little awkward, he was making a drink. He looked around and saw it was me, "Your Mother told me about you and Susan, its good you're supporting her". And again, that was it.

Telling Susan's parents wasn't what we had planned, I met Sue near to where she lived and as we were walking I was telling her about my parents.

I said to her "Come on, we'll tell your Mum and Dad now".

"Too late" she said, "I've already told them" and she had. When we walked through the door her Mum came straight towards me, all 6ft of her.

"Are you going to support her? If you're not you can go now and we will take care of the baby"

I'm sure I must have been trembling, I said to her "I'm staying". Mary was Susan's Mum and Dennis her Dad, they were hard working, struggling but very welcoming. Mary was a great cook, she could make great meals from virtually nothing. The majority of food was on `Tic`, which meant it was written down by the shop keeper and the customer would pay for it at the end of the week. It was common practice at that time.

Sue and I decided to make a date to get married before the birth so we went on the bus to the registry office to discuss the event. I needed my birth certificate and Sue needed hers. The Registrar in the Town Hall took my application and before long she came back."You were not born here love" she said, "not in Barnsley! I suggest you go back to see your parents and ask them".

I telephoned my Mum, "Hey up Mum, this woman at the Town Hall said I should speak to you because I wasn't born here in Barnsley". My Mum told me to come home and we'd sort it out, thinking there had been an obvious mistake we'd made. My Mum and Dad were both in the kitchen waiting; I told them what had been said at the Town Hall. My Mum looked worried, "Well, it's probably a good time to tell you your Dad's not your real Dad and your surname is Evans not Smith". Well you could have knocked me over with a laced handbag, I couldn't believe it. Well, I could really because a few months earlier I was trying to nick a fiver from my Dad's suit pocket when I spotted their marriage certificate. I looked at it out of curiosity and it stated that both my parents had previously been married and they had both been divorced. I kind of knew something wasn't right. What still makes me laugh is my Mum blamed Susan, accusing her of `egging me on` to snoop around. As far as I was concerned they had kept this secret without telling a soul. It made no difference to me, `Derek` was my dad, I knew no other and he'd done a sterling job so far.

My only disappointment really was worrying what Jason would think because he was Derek's son. He was my half brother effectively; I need not have worried as he is fine about it all. David was altogether different, a typical drama queen. He went off on one and ran away to his girlfriend's but everything settled back down. We had to legally change our names to Smith via a solicitor and then 'finally' we booked the wedding.

In sickness and in health...apparently.

"I'm going to wear FUCKING Black" Sue said to me. My Mum was uncomfortable with Sue wearing white, what with her being five months gone. I don't think my Mum meant it but my future wife did, "I'll wear what I like, it's nobody's business" and she was right. Sue's sister and partner were providing us with a car, I had him as best man also which was strange because I barely knew him. The White Heart pub had been booked for the night time celebrations and in the afternoon we had a meal in the local snooker club.

The meal was very nice from what I remember, my parents and new in-laws were there, my grandparents also and brothers and sisters from both sides. My Granddad made us all laugh, he was leaning over the plate eating his salad except it wasn't salad. My Gran said "Fred, you're eating your button hole!", he laughed about it, well we all did. In the middle of the room was the wedding cake. It was huge and beautiful, my Grandparents had bought it. We had a bread van in Yorkshire called `Fletchers` and my Gran had got this beautiful cake from there on the `never never`, which means she had to pay a little week by week. A good year later I was visiting my Grandparents when the Fletchers van beeped his horn. My Gran grabbed her purse and we went out to buy some goodies.

Whilst in the van and in front of her neighbours, the man said "Are you gonna pay off that cake Nellie?"

"I'm bloody not" she told him. "It was crap, there was a big air bubble in the middle and we only got a few decent pieces out of it".

I never knew whether she ended up paying for it but I didn't care, the cake was lovely just like my Grandmother.

I'll be honest with you and say I wasn't in love with Susan, I loved her but I wasn't *in* love. This wasn't Susan's fault, it was in my head. I just knew things weren't right but she was pregnant and I wasn't going to leave her alone. Daniel was born on the 6th March 1988, weighing 9lb 7oz, a big baby and still is. I was eating a Cadbury's Cream Egg whilst she was in labour. I had just offered some to Susan in-between her contractions, surprisingly she declined.

The nurse caring for Sue and the baby said "Do you want to have a look and maybe feel his head?"

"No," I said "when he's washed and in clean clothes I'll look at him".

Poor Susan had gone through a long ordeal, she was knackered and I was stuffed. I telephoned my Mum to say it was a boy and timed it just right; my Dad had just come in from a Sunday afternoon at the Sportsman Pub. Mum told me that as soon as she told him it was a boy, he just burst out into tears over his Sunday lunch, bless him. It was the first grandchild on both sides so it was very emotional for all of us.

I was temporarily staying at Mum's, poor Susan was still in hospital and the new baby we called `Daniel` had been allowed home with me for a few days until Susan was well again. All the parents were proud but Mary (Susan's mum) was especially proud, I could see it from day one. Even my dad would take Daniel out for a walk in the pram, for a tough northern man this was amazing to me but we all fell in love with him. He was our first born. The council gave us a two bedroom house on Newhill Road, near my parents. Soon afterwards we were a family, all three of us in our own little house.

I don't know what was wrong with me at that time but I never worked, I contemplated looking for work but it never happened. It wasn't mentioned by anyone so I stayed on the dole. My parents had always worked, Susan's parents were working but me, no. To this day I'll never understand why.

My parents soon sold the betting shop and decided they wanted to move, they decided to live in Skegness, Lincolnshire. Whilst they were looking around the properties in skeggy, my Aunty Pam and her family decided they would move with them. They left my brother David in charge of the house. Wrong thing really, he was so in love with a girl in Doncaster that he didn't want to keep coming back to check on the house. A few days before they set off they bought a Touring caravan and over the next few days or so I watched my Mum and Aunty Pam turn this shell into a beautiful mobile home. My Aunty Pam is a great Seamstress and she could sew anything. New curtains all round, new furnishings, the best of the best all recycled from our house. The big day arrived, the Ford Cortina Estate and 4 adults all comfortable in the car, Jason and Glynn squashed in between. They were off, with all their possessions stored equally in the Tourer. Glen told me the other side of Louth there is a big long series of hills, the final one being the worst. He said the Cortina struggled with them all and he had to take it steady, dropping a gear to get over the hill. On the last hill, near the top he had to drop into first gear. He looked around to the passengers and said "We are in the lowest gear, we can't drop anymore". She made it and they all sighed a huge relief.

It didn't take long for Susan to fall pregnant again, this time it was more difficult. The hospital warned her things could be difficult and she may need a caesarian section. If I remember correctly she did go into labour but eventually they went down to theatre. When Jason was born he had a broken clavicle and a collapsed lung. He was in hospital for 10 days. We had moved to a different house, Cherry's road, it was a three bedroom council house, nearer to Susan's parents. The frustration was definitely playing with my head; me and Susan were always arguing and fighting. I'm ashamed to say I'd go wild and punch out but Susan was a Barnsley lass and knew how to fight back. It's no excuse, we were kids with 2 kids. We stayed there for a while but I was getting itchy feet so we decided to join my parents in Skegness It wasn't easy for Sue to leave her parents and they weren't too happy we were moving but we convinced them it was a good move and they would always have free holidays. The seaside didn't help our relationship; we were living in hotel rooms, a caravan and the last few months in a Bed and Breakfast. I actually got off my arse in Skegness and I found work on the fairground, every day I had to walk past The Embassy Theatre. That year in Skegness Norman Wisdom was playing his show. Who would have thought a couple of years later I'd be meeting him at his home on the Isle of Man.

I didn't have a driving license and I didn't really own a car. Owning a car means paying for its maintenance, Insurance, Tax and MOT. I had an Austin maxi, I loved the car but I had none of the required documents to drive legally. The car had no Tax, I used to go to the scrap yard to find a 6th month or 9th month tax disc, cut out the number and turn it upside down, a 6 made a 9 and a 9 made a 6. I was in the `Ship` car park one day when this police car shot into the car park and pulled up in front of me, I panicked as I had my home made tax disc in the window. He must have heard about my enterprise because he went straight to the passenger door and tried to open it. I was too quick; I grabbed the tax disc and as the copper was looking at me through the glass, I shoved it in my mouth and started chewing. Yeah, I had eaten it. The copper was quite shocked, I expected a big telling off but he just smirked and asked me why I'd done it. I told him "I don't know what you're talking about. The car's not taxed that's why it's in the car park". He couldn't do or say anything so he left.

My parents broke up whilst living in Skegness, Mum got an apartment on her own and Dad lived in the same annex he had rented with mother. Jason, my brother, stayed with my Dad. Things were getting tense with Susan, we weren't in love. We loved the kids but we were starting to hurt each other verbally and mentally. After a few phone calls to Susan's parents we decided to move back to Barnsley and after living with the in-laws for a few weeks, we found a house in the town centre. We set up home again and got on with being parents. The routine was the same, the only difference was we were visiting the in-laws more and Susan was spending more time with her sisters. They would often go out drinking together and as we were in the town centre it was easier for them to walk to our home. One night I was waiting for their return and it was gone 12. I could hear some arguing up the street, it was the girls returning. I stood on the step looking towards the figures when I heard Susan's sister say "If you don't shut up, I'll tell Steve everything". Obviously, I wanted to know what the secret was and I confronted them when they got into the house. It turned out my wife had been shagging my best mate that night behind the Odeon cinema in town, not only that but it had happened before. I was shocked. I'll admit to not really blaming her, I wasn't sexually active with Susan in the final months but I never expected her to have an affair. It was the excuse I needed.

A New Beginning.

The next morning I packed my stuff, said goodbye to the kids and drove to Skegness. I was crying all the way. I never blamed Susan for the break up, I wasn't happy and neither was she, we were destroying each other. I didn't show any interest in Susan and she was an attractive girl, this other guy did. Truth be known, I was discovering myself and I decided that from that day onwards I would be open and strong and tell people I was GAY. Yeah I know what you're thinking, it took me long enough. It did take a long time for me to figure it out but deep down I knew and now I had to live with it. My friends say I merely turned to the Dark Side or that I was on the 'bisexual bus'. I wasn't and now I had to start again.

Apart from exploring my new life I was also dealing with my parents break up, Dad had driven miles to try and find Mum. Mum was only down the road but he didn't know. Mum was dating a man called `Pete`, he was the manager of the Ship hotel. They had been secretly dating and even I had no idea. I got a phone call one day from my brother, "Come round to the annex Steve, Dad needs you". I went round and the worst had happened, my Grandmother Smith had passed away. My poor Dad was heartbroken, we all were. I went round to tell my Mum and she came round to help us consol my Dad. My Grandmother Smith was an important woman to me, she was the head of her family. She was a great laugh, very funny, sometimes scary and I knew we would all miss her, we still do. I never went to her funeral, I can't even tell you why. I've regretted it ever since. I should have been there for my dad, he needed me but as usual I was tied up in my own little world.

I was struggling in Skegness to find people like myself, it seemed like I was literally `the only gay in the village`. There was one bar but it was full of fat old men and I wasn't thrilled with it all. I did have a friend Belinda and she introduced me to Alan, he was a male prostitute. We had a few drinks together and I soon realised he was a bit weird. He told me in a few weeks he was going to Leicester to do some decorating at a friend's house, he invited me to help out for a bit of cash. I said "Yeah, why not!" I was sorted for a room in Skegness, I went back to the Bed and Breakfast I had stayed at before with Sue. It was clean and tidy, 2 pairs of pants, one on and one off and drying on the radiator, it was classy. I was doing little jobs here and there. In summer, I was running the car park scam, along with Pete at the Ship. I would put signs out stating the seafront car parks were full and we charged a quid to park, it was split 50/50 between us. I was a bugger for fiddling £20 for myself and sometimes more. I made a good living through summer and Pete had a good side line.

The time had come for me and Alan to go to Leicester to decorate his friend's house. The house was being converted to flats with the downstairs flat for the 'friend'. The 'friend' had bought loads of furniture in Skeggy and I was expected to help him get it delivered and upstairs. The shop had provided a van and a driver. I got up that morning and helped out in the café for a free breakfast (My B&B also had a café above), I put my mail in my bag and went to meet them. Everything was loaded but there were only two seats so Alan asked if I'd mind getting into the back of the van with the `friend` and we would swap halfway. I agreed and as there was a couch I sat down, it was pitch black except for the broken light. The `friend` turned out to be a goggle eyed, fat and sweaty looking man and his eyes never left me in that van. He just ignored my attempt for any conversation, I tried to take a kip but he took that as an invitation to try his hand. I was desperately trying to engage him into conversation at the same time moving away, even climbing over the furniture and then back to the couch (it was like a Benny Hill film), and all the time without a word. It was scary but finally he gave up, short of breath and sweating like a farm animal, he sat down. Luckily we pulled in for a coffee and I jumped out and gave Alan a right bollocking. "I'm in the front now" I said to him, he reluctantly agreed and we arrived maybe 40 minutes later. Leicester, a city I had never been to before, I loved it already.

The house was horrid, red gloss paint on every skirting board and doorway, the banister also bright red, the walls in every room were matt sky blue, you can imagine. It only took a few whiskies all round for me to realise I had been brought here for more than decorating and to make things worst there was only one big bed. Bedtime was hell, my hell. I was in a situation; I'm good at this, getting myself into situations. It was early hours and I was between fatty and the Hustler, I felt one hand come one way and another hand come the other and they both started to grope me. I wasn't having any of it, I didn't mind Alan, he was quite cute but I wasn't doing this. I waited a minute (or two) then pretended to wake up startled, jumped out of the bed and went into the lounge.

Alan came after me, "What's the matter? You'll make some good money".

"No Alan" I said, "I can't do this and it's not for me".

He took a bottle from the mantle, "Here sniff this" he said passing me a bottle. "It will make you feel better".

I took a big sniff and I thought my head and heart were going to explode. I couldn't breathe so I got up and sat on the door step outside, Alan just shook his head and went back to bed. That night I slept on the settee but I didn't really sleep, I was too worried I was going to die. It was a bottle of Poppers and I do not recommend it. The next morning my two so called 'friends' were acting like nothing had happened, I woke to a coffee and a bacon sandwich. I asked about the decorating and Alan said we were going to forget it for today, instead we were going to a Gay bar in Leicester, The Dover Castle. Fatty was staying behind, probably planning his next move on me.

We walked into Leicester and went to this Gay bar, there were a few guys in, a coloured lad behind the bar was quite cute I thought. There was music playing on TV, something like MTV. We got a drink and within minutes Alan said "I'm drinking this and I'm off down the road to The Pineapple", another gay pub. He asked if I was going to join him but I said "No, I'll stay here and wait for you to come back, I've got to get used to these places". He said goodbye and told me he'd be back in about an hour or so.

So there I was, in a Gay bar on my own for the first time. I decided to get another beer and try to look cool, I was rummaging through my bag and found my mail I had brought with me from Skegness. Some of it was crap but I opened one looking official and it was my Divorce, my decree absolute. I couldn't believe it, my first gay bar and I'm divorced. I decided on another drink to celebrate. For some time this lad had been watching me, he had dark eyes, sexy skin and stubble. As I approached the bar he said "Hi". I said hello back to him, inside I was shaking. I asked him if he'd like a drink, I couldn't believe my own nerve. Luckily he accepted a beer. I learnt his name was Simon and he'd just called in for a few drinks, apparently he had come in after me and sat at the bar. I hadn't noticed him but he had me, he said I looked new and nervous.

Here we go again.

It was a few hours before I realised that I was pissed, Alan wasn't back and the new lad could drink. He was a very thirsty man so we moved onto another bar and after more alcohol we decided he should come and live with me in Skegness. Yeah, I was a quick charmer. We got on the train to Melton Mowbray where he lived with an older man. There was no one in the house when we got there so he packed all his stuff including his small change box and we got back on the train to Leicester. We went to fatties place to get my stuff, Alan was home and didn't seem to be bothered that he'd left me behind. I explained the situation; I was going home and asked fatty for my train fare. He refused. I mentioned I would report him to the cops and he gave me £16. By this time, it was quite late and dark. We walked to the coach station then to the railway station, we found the train to Grantham. We worked out we may only have enough for one of us to get to Skegness so we planned to get to Grantham and try and thumb our way to Skegness. In Grantham we were told we'd missed the last train, the next one was 6am. The guard told us we couldn't sleep on the station so we bedded down in the long grass outside. We were literally yards from the ticket office, it was cold but dry. As we got settled Simon tried to grab my willy, I wasn't amused so he went off to try and find a 24hr garage for some drinks. He was gone over an hour and I assumed he had gone back to Leicester but no, he came back with a drink and we tried to settle down to sleep. At about 2am there was a noise, then shouting and these two lads ran straight past me and Simon, they dropped something as they dived over the fencing. We couldn't see what they had dropped but we could see the police so we stayed put, we didn't want to get involved.

As it was getting light we got all our money together including Simon's change box and we discovered we had enough for two tickets to Skeggy and two coffees. There was a little money left over which Simon used for 10 fags. We paid for the tickets with the change and paid for the coffees and fags in 5ps and coppers. The owner of the café was quite suspicious of us, it transpired that the lads running away had broken in to the café and stole all her change including a box of fags. She told us they had dropped a sleeve as they jumped the fence, we missed out there. We boarded the train but it wasn't to be, the police boarded and came over to sit with us. They obviously thought we had done the robbery. They held the train up for 5 minutes, questioning us in front of everyone and then they left, quite happy that we had nothing to do with it all. Thank god they believed us. I never saw fatty or Alan again. We arrived in Skegness early morning. We went round to the B&B I was staying at and I introduced Si to the landlady but to be honest, we just needed a shower and some sleep.

Left with a wife, came back with a boyfriend.

Mum was still living at the hotel with Pete, I introduced my new boyfriend and she was cool about it all. "Don't flaunt yourself around" she said. "There's no need for it."
Things didn't go well for us from the start, we were constantly getting drunk and fighting and I mean real fighting, then getting drunk again. We were camping it up in straight bars, the worst bit for me was all the married men I knew, who after a few drinks would come and join us to tell us their secrets. "I'm gay but my wife doesn't know", they would brag. I hated this, why burden me? Go and be a fucking man, tell your wife, stop wasting other people's time and ruining lives.

We were drunk again but this time I had an excuse. My brother David's little baby boy had been still born, poor David and Kay, they were devastated. Simon and I decided to get drunk and we became emotional then violent towards each other and on the way home we started fighting. I went to punch Si, decided not to and instead punched a window which smashed, I was in the nick. The police found me walking the streets with blood all over my hands, Simon had run off. In the local nick I started to sober quickly and soon asked for a solicitor. Whilst I was talking to the solicitor I could hear shouting," Steve, is that you? I love you". It was Simon in the next cell, I could have died of embarrassment. I was new to all this and didn't expect to be `ousted` in the police cells. We were let out a few hours later, we walked to the garage got some fags and went home. The police had been and the landlady wasn't happy so the next day we moved out into a 6 berth caravan further up the street. This is where I saw my first GHOST.

The caravan was great, it was private, cozy and we loved it. It didn't have a full size bed in the bedroom but within days the landlady had bought us a second hand one from the church. I couldn't wait to sleep in a real bed in our new home and this time we didn't celebrate, Simon had a few beers but really we were enjoying the privacy. We were looking after a lovely golden retriever for the landlady and the dog was in the bedroom on his bed. In the middle of the night I woke and at the bottom of the bed, just standing there was a lady, all in black with 1930's style clothing. She didn't look scary or angry, she just looked at me and started walking through the door into the main living area. As she did the dog jumped, started barking and followed her. By the time I'd woke Si and we were in the lounge, the lady had gone. The dog was still agitated and sniffing around the floor. Before you make an assumption, I can assure you I wasn't dreaming and I wasn't drunk. I was as awake as I am now typing this and what I saw I couldn't explain. It was the first ghost I'd ever seen but it wasn't to be the last. We kind of stole a car, not really stole but `acquired`. This guy said we could buy it for £100, £20 a week. We paid him one payment and drove to the bar. We said goodbye to Mum and Pete, we were on an adventure, to travel a little and settle somewhere. We eventually settled in Brighton.

This part of my memory is quite vague but somehow we ended up living on Viaduct road, a basement room, well two actually, one as a lounge and one as a bedroom. We shared the toilet/bathroom with other tenants and we all had one big kitchen between us. The whole house was on a pre-pay electricity meter, we had to pay £22 a month, taking it in turns to charge the key. We had kept the dog from Skegness, I think the landlady was glad we'd taken him. We soon got around all the gay bars in Brighton, my favourite being `The Marlborough` theatre bar. Chris was the owner, I got on very well with him and we used to chat a lot. We were extremely poor, living on only dole money. We would sleep all day and spend the early hours of most morning nicking milk, eggs, bread, anything we could get hold of. The only time we slept at night was the night before we signed on, we'd be there very early to sign and collect a cheque each.

Back then if you lived in rooms like us, it was classed as an unsafe address and you could collect your dole money. It wasn't long before the guys upstairs hated two puffs living below and they would piss in buckets and throw it on our washing line of clothes or throw stuff at the dog, screaming threats to us.

Whilst using the kitchen one day, I left our food for a minute. When I went back to dish up the grub, it was Sausage and Mash, they had sprinkled glass into our mashed potato. Simon went berserk and went upstairs to argue it out but the guys had a knife and the lad directly above tried to break our door down to stab us. We got outside with the dog and went to the police; they said they would come out so we sat on the steps outside for 3 hours until they came. They heard our story and went upstairs to see the guys, we could hear them all laughing upstairs, including the cops. They came back down and told us there isn't a problem, the guys are fine with us and we shouldn't worry. Shortly after the police had left, the shouting and banging had started again and we decided enough was enough. I telephoned my brother David and asked for help, he agreed to pick us up and drop us in `Stratford upon Avon`, where Simon's parents lived. I didn't see what Simon did to the rooms we rented but I believe he shit and pissed everywhere. I trashed the food in the kitchen and as I was leaving I grabbed the prepay electricity key and put it in my pocket. David turned up as planned and we got our gear in the car. I threw the prepay key onto the M25, laughing to myself knowing it was Friday night and by the time they realised, it would be too late and they would have no electricity until Monday.

An Ultimatum

Thanks to David we were safely in Stratford, Simon's parents took us in although we had to get rid of the dog. He went to a farm. Things were ok, we had free board and lodgings and Christmas was coming. We all got drunk a lot and I made the mistake of telling them my stories of tax disc forgery and driving illegally After a big fight over Christmas time, Simon's parents gave Simon an ultimatum, "You can stay but only if you ditch the puff."

I thought he'd support me but he didn't, he told me it was easier if I left and that he would lose his family if I didn't.

I had a suitcase and about £5 cash, I walked to a nearby church and knocked on the vicarage door. Two men came to the door, one looked like a Vicar and the other must have been a friend. I asked if they could help me, I was homeless and I had very little money, the Vicar apologised and told me he couldn't help. I was more than annoyed; I only wanted a bed for the night. I set off walking the 7 miles to Stratford town centre, I thought at least there I'll be relatively safe. I had walked about half way when a car beeped at me, it was dark but as the car pulled alongside I recognised the Vicar's mate. He offered me a lift to Stratford. He also offered me some money to suck his cock but I declined. The journey was only minutes thank god because I don't know who was more embarrassed, him or me. I thanked him and had a walk around the town. I set up camp underneath a debt collection agency, high rise building. They had a shed with a roof; it was their smoking area and underneath the main building so it was dry. I got my suitcase open, took out my pink quilt and put on some clean clothes I left everything in the smoking area and went to a local gay pub Simon had told me about.

The Queens Head was on Ely street, nice little quaint pub. I bought a drink and sat in the corner, no change there then. Like most gay bars, it wasn't long before the bravest 'queen' came over to talk to me. I told him my story, gave him the full sympathy tale. He bought me a drink and then his mate bought me a drink and before long I was entertaining the whole bar with my tales of woe. Coincidently a Vicar came into the bar and after hearing my story he cornered me and slipped £20 in my hand. "Meet me at the clock tower at 12", he said. I took the cash. Just before closing time this lad invited me to join him the next morning for breakfast in a café he worked in. I agreed and thanked him. It was about 11.40 and I was heading towards the tower, not to meet the Vicar but it was near my new temporary home. I got a scare when someone tapped me on the shoulder, it was the Vicar.

"Don't forget Steve, 12 o'clock at the clock tower. Will you be there?" he asked holding on to my £20 I said "Yeah I'll be there, you'll recognise me. I'll be the one sat in the back of the police car pointing to you"

He just looked at me and walked off. What is it with me and Vicars?

I had a lovely cozy nights sleep and woke up warm, dry and with £20 quid in my pocket. I made a decision that morning, I was going to find somewhere to live and get a job. The police station was local so I went down to them and introducing myself I explained my situation. They told me to go to a guest house near the railway station. A guy called John answered the door. I lied and told him I was working in a café and needed a room, he gave me the smallest room in the house but I wasn't complaining. I went into the town and tried for a few jobs but one in particular caught my eye, it was called `The Hathaway Tearooms'. I enquired about the vacancy, the Manageress was called Marge. I knew immediately she'd be a tough old cookie and she was.

In the interview she said, "Be aware I can be a bitch if you get my back up"

I looked into her eyes and said "I can be a bigger bitch but I will work hard for you".

The tension was there but good old Marge, she gave me the job anyway, I think she considered me a challenge. I wanted a job and somewhere to live and I'd done it, in about eight hours.

That afternoon I was in Stratford when I saw Simon getting off a bus, he saw me, waved and came over. I was a bit `off` I have to admit but it was also nice to see a face I recognised and I did have a story to tell. We went to the pub with my £20 (cheers vicar), we got drunk, I managed to smuggle Si into the bed and breakfast and he stayed the night. I started to see him again and with my new job I was soon able to afford a better place to live. We found a new apartment and I moved out of the B&B as soon as possible. Some weeks later, the owner John was arrested for running a brothel. I'd seen girls in there and I did wonder why I was the only one for breakfast but I never saw any action. I missed out really.

Mum and Pete were moving out of the hotel in Skegness, they were offered a pub in Tutbury, nr Burton upon Trent. The pub was called `The Castle'; it was old, run down and boring but I knew my

Mum and Pete would bring it back to life. I approached my Mum and Pete to see if I could borrow some money to buy a car, a Y-reg Fiesta. She was a good little runner and after taking Pete out for a run in it, he agreed she was a good purchase and lent me the money. Working at Hathaway's was great, I was working with Chris, Les and Val. We are all still friends today, twenty years on. Three girls and me, we made a good team. Simon got a job a few doors down from us, he was at the `Shakespeare Hotel` and his position was Porter. I always did well in tips and I'd go over to the hotel for a posh coffee. It was great to sit in front of a beautiful lounge fire with a coffee and free biscuits. It wasn't cheap though, £7 a time, so the biscuits weren't that free!

I was quite popular at Hathaway's with staff and customers. The American customers were great, we had big glass cabinets of homemade cakes and I'd show them a full tray to tempt them. I would leave the tray of cakes and go to make their drinks, winking at them "I'll trust you with the cakes, if any disappear it's not my fault." I would go into the kitchen and return five minutes later, sure enough a few cakes would have gone, probably in tissue in their bags. When it came to the bill I would wink again, saying "I think I've got everything" and give them the bill. I made on average £20 a day in tips which was bloody good in 1991.

I was getting restless again and my mum had asked us if we'd like to move into the pub, no rent or bills but helping out in the bar. We decided to do it and we did, everything thrown in the Fiesta and we were off, no notice given, nothing.

Fireworks at 'The Castle`.

Living in a pub was stupid for me and Simon, beer on tap, but we enjoyed the company and new family. Lynne and Debbie were also living there, Pete's daughters. His son Chris came to visit with his footballers friends. I looked forward to their visits, especially as some of these footballers got very drunk and one got his willy out. I wanted to get the camera but as I looked around my Mum was already on the floor underneath this footballer and taking pictures of his tackle, we couldn't get a look in. She's a dirty bitch.

I painted that pub inside and out. Actually we all painted it but sucker me was the only one at the top of the ladder, 28 feet high, painting the exterior in glorious sunshine. I must have been mad but we needed the money. Talking about money, we weren't earning very much at the pub so I got a job in a fireworks factory, `Cosmic Fireworks`. Every day I would come home covered in gun powder and Simon would flick his lighter threatening to burn me. If he'd have done it I'd have gone up like Guy Fawkes.

It was 'that time' again, we were bored living in a pub so we wanted out and got a little apartment a few yards down the road in Hatton. We were very close to the `Nestles` chocolate and coffee factory, I used to dribble like Homer Simpson when I could smell the chocolate cooking. The whole area smelt like freshly brewed coffee every morning, I loved it. We had a neighbour, a single bloke and quite cute but very private. We used to chat and once he came round for a drink. On the other side of us were a young family, we said hello every day but really we spent a lot of our time in the pub visiting the family and drinking the free ale. The whole village was on alert one week; a woman had been attacked whilst walking her dogs and one the week after, two attempted rapes in two weeks. We made sure my Mum, Lynne and Debbie were all escorted if they went to the shops and the village locals kept an eye on their neighbours, especially if they were single or elderly. The week we moved out of that apartment, I picked up a local paper and on the front page was a picture of the guy they suspected, it was our cute neighbour. I read on and apparently he'd been questioned by the police and when they went back to question him again, he had wired his wrists to the mains cooker and switched it on. He was dead in the kitchen when they found him, I couldn't believe it. Why would a good looking, smart looking and successful guy resort to raping for a kick? He could have dated any woman he wanted! It astounded me and it proves that you never really know your neighbours.

Yes, you read it right, we moved again. Mum and Pete had been offered a different pub and we decided to stay so we moved into Burton on Trent. This was a nice house, quite big and furnished. We had a dog, a small black bitch called Kirsty and she was a bitch, literally! As soon as you turned your back, she'd destroy anything in sight. I was now working as a Security Guard, looking after the warehouses for Bass Brewery. It was a night shift so I walked around like a zombie most days. One night a driver called in to see me, he'd got three puppies who were free to a good home so he asked if I wanted one. I said yes and chose one; he was a beautiful cross breed. I was hoping the new puppy would calm Kirsty down but that was a mistake. We also had two budgies and two Zebra Finch. The job was quite a challenge, a challenge to stay awake it was that boring. One night I called the police and told them someone was trying to break into the wagons, they were there in minutes. I also rang head office to assure them I hadn't seen them but with all the activity my night flew by. Another occasion I went into the main office and sat down for just a minute. Four hours later I woke up, startled I ran back to the cabin just in time to issue passes to the drivers, phew.

I was quite inquisitive and enjoyed looking around the ware-houses. In one of them I stepped back in dismay as I looked at a room full of neatly piled cans of beer and lager, 120 feet high. There were thousands and thousands of cans and it looked like heaven. I heard a noise in one corner and walked over. One of the drivers had used a forklift truck to get to the top of a pile where he was sitting, drink-ing beer. I climbed up and he nearly shit himself when he saw me. "Don't worry" I said, "I'll join you" and I opened a beer. We chatted for a while and we drunk a few more, then without a word this driver unzipped his trousers and got his cock out. He started masturbating in front of me. I watched until he'd finished, he didn't apologise or look embarrassed. He just cleaned himself up, thanked me, patted my shoulder and left. I was stunned. The next night I saw him again, he was near one of the trucks. I walked up to say hi and I must have scared him. He swung around, grabbing me by the neck and pushed me against a truck. He started to feel my cock through my trousers but just as I started to enjoy it he stopped. I hadn't seen anyone but over my shoulder was another driver, he was coming towards us. He asked the other guy if I was `cosha` and he nodded. They moved closer together and played with each other in front of me. I could have walked away and I wasn't particularly interested but I just stood there watching. I was fascinated by how blatant they were.

One of my last night's working there was near Christmas time. In the early hours of the morning, some of the drivers were talking in the canteen. They told me that every year they knocked over a pile of these cans, pretending it was an accident. Then they would fill their cars with beer, Guinness and lager. When everyone had got their share, they would ring security to say what had happened, he would report it and nobody seemed to care. The drivers asked if I'd be up for it. I thought about it, for about 3 seconds, and said yes. I was told to go and get my car and reverse it up to the other drivers' cars but as I got out of the car I heard the most amazing crash. The sound was coming from the warehouse. All the drivers stood back as some of the breached cans exploded their load everywhere and in every direction. A minute or so later, everything was calm and we all filled our cars with free cans, some were sticky but who cared, it was free. I counted over 400 cans and Simon was thrilled. A good Christmas all round.

I needed to sort something out; I started to notice blood when I went to the loo. I ignored it for a while but it was causing stomach cramps so I made an appointment with the doctor. When I attended the surgery I was getting nervous, not for my complaint but how to describe it and then I realised the doctor must have seen it all before so I blurted it out. He checked me over and said I probably had piles. I knew he was wrong but when a doctor tells you something you kind of trust them.

We sold our car and bought a Transit Camper Van. It was old and had oil leaks but it had everything inside, seats, a bed, a cooker and a fridge so we set about doing it up. It was about this time that my Dad and brother came to visit. It was the first time my Dad had come to any of my houses and I was thrilled to see them. We went to the pub, I took him around the town and showed him the sights and then we went back home to eat. I was opening some post there and Dad noticed the envelope; I'd forgotten to tell him I had changed my surname to Simon's surname, Savage. He never said anything but I knew he was hurt. The truth is I had always known inside I wasn't a 'Smith' and my birth name 'Evans' didn't feel right either. I used Simon's surname because it was convenient and a happy medium. Simon's parents came to visit us also. We did the usual routine, had a meal, showed them the town and went back for coffee before their journey home. Simon and his dad went into the house first whilst we took our shopping out of the car. The look on Simon's face told me something was wrong. I went inside but they wouldn't let me in to the back room. The `bitch` dog had got hold of the birds and killed them, literally pulled the feathers off them, it was an evil sight. We'd left some washing up in the sink, floating inside were the Finches. The dog had scared them half to death in her `rampage` and she had broken open their cage. We can only assume that in their panic they flew into the water and drowned, I was devastated.

Within days we had packed the van and we were off. "What about Scotland?" I asked as we drove north. After staying the night on a camp site, the next day we arrived on the outskirts of Edinburgh. At that point we changed our minds and we wanted to go back to Brighton again, so we set off back south. In Barnsley, there's a very steep hill called `Harborough hill`. As I child I would often use my shoes as brakes as I came down the hill on my bicycle. This time we were going up it in the van. Having traveled all the way back from Edinburgh, we got half way up the hill when there was a massive bang and white smoke billowing everywhere, we'd blown something. The AA came out to rescue us, they ended up taking us to Simon's parents in Stratford Upon Avon. I was back, two years after they had thrown me out. I wasn't giving them the chance again so within days the van was scrapped and I bought a Skoda. We set off for Brighton and the journey was sweet until we hit the M25. Not far from the M4 exit, we were in the outside lane doing about 70 mph and all of a sudden, `BANG!` This time it filled the whole car with smoke. I swerved across four lanes, luckily everyone could see what had happened and they let me through as the car was still rolling. I lifted the bonnet and there was a big hole in the side of the engine. I asked the AA guy if he could repair it, he told me it was scrap.

Back to where I began.

We were towed to Brighton where the car was scrapped. The first thing we had to do was get rid of the dogs, it sounds cruel I know but it was obvious we were incapable of keeping them and no one wanted tenants with dogs. The local council dog warden came out immediately and took the dogs, he was a nice guy and he understood why we had no choice. We found a room in Bedford Square, it was rough and dirty and the toilet was on the landing for everyone to use. It was mounted a foot from the floor on a big wooden stand with no carpet or seat, I didn't expect luxury but good god, I expected better. I thought this place was the Gay capital?

The first night, the neighbours above became rock stars. At about 3am, they threw their TV out of the bedroom window, it hit our window sill and fell three floors down to the street with a huge explosion. The next day we moved out. I had found an advert for a Studio apartment, it sounded good and reasonably priced so we made an appointment to view it. The landlord was a very smart looking Asian gentleman. He showed us around the studio, it was tiny but we needed somewhere. The landlord was quizzing us and asking questions, I could see he was trying to work us out. Just as I thought he was stalling, to get rid of us he said "Look guys, I have an apartment on Marine square. It has a sea view and I'm looking for some good tenants for it. It's a bit more expensive but I think you'll both love it. Do you want to see it?" We said yes. Yes Please!

We moved into Marine Square, it was a second floor, one bedroom apartment. Very clean and tidy, quite modern and with a sea view, it felt quite exclusive. The landlord was a nice guy, he gave us everything we needed and we were happy to live there. My bowel problems were starting to affect me in a big way. Blood in the toilet again and I could barely walk more than ¼ of a mile without feeling like I was going to faint. I made an appointment with a new GP who told me I had IBS, I was given creams and pills but they didn't really help. We bought an Austin Allegro, `Vanden Plas`. It had a big grill like a Rolls Royce on the front, she drove as rough as a petrol lawn mower. We often drove to Yorkshire to see my Dad and Jason, they were now living in a small apartment at the top of a Victorian house in Barnsley centre. It was a great little apartment. Every time we visited my Dad and Jason we would end up in a local bar `The Wilthorpe`. We would get pissed and go back for my Dad to cook us some burgers, he makes a mean cheeseburger. We also went to see Simon's parents, they were having a few problems. Literally just after we arrived, their other son had come out as being gay, for the book I'll call him `T`. By the time we had set off back home to Brighton, T had asked if he could come and live with us in a few weeks or so, we said "Yeah, no problem".

We had been shopping in Brighton centre, walking home through kemp town when Simon said "That's Dora Bryan behind us. She's from some of the Victoria Wood shows we have seen on TV and she was in some Norman Wisdom films." I looked back to see her, we slowed down and I turned quickly to ask her for an autograph, half scaring her to death. She was really friendly and we chatted for a short while. Simon spoke more than me because he knew her work more. We discovered she was our neighbour. Her back garden backed onto our bit. We started to talk through the bedroom window when Dora was in her garden. As Simon was working, I used to chat with her for ten or fifteen minutes at a time. I was a Norman Wisdom fan and I hadn't realised it was Dora in his films. She had a big parrot which flew freely in her back garden. I would watch as it amused itself with a watering can, throwing it around and ducking its head.

We decided one day to walk into town. As we got onto the seafront my stomach started cramping, I was doubled over with blood pouring down my leg, I couldn't move. Simon got me home and I just stood in the bedroom with blood and shit all down my legs, I was in agony. Things settled down but I was feeling rough so I walked around the corner to the doctor's surgery, I nearly fainted on the door step.

I crawled through the door and looked at the receptionist, "I need help, I need to see a doctor."
She looked at me and asked "Are you registered here?"
"No, but I need to see someone urgently" I replied.
She stood up and looked at me through the glass partition. "No, I'm sorry but we don't deal with drug addicts here. You'll have to go to the hospital", and with that she sat back down.
I pleaded with her with tears in my eyes but she was a stern bitch, I left. I had just got through the door when I fell to my knees, blood everywhere. Simon got hold of me, nothing seemed to faze him, blood, crap, it didn't matter. He took me to the bedroom and called

my GP. He came within the hour and within the next 30 minutes I was in an ambulance and in hospital. They prodded and poked me, gave me pills, fluids and blood tests and after the indignity of a camera up my back passage, they told me I had Ulcerative Colitis, which meant nothing to me. They also said my blood level was 6.4 and it should be between 12 and 13, so I needed 5 units of blood. The doctor came to see me the next day, I was half way through the transfusion. "You're lucky to be here, you could have had a heart attack at any time. Why did you wait?" he said. I told him I had seen various doctors. Within no time I was feeling great. I went home after three days and I was pink, not pale. We celebrated in the pub.

Strange things happen when you've been ill. I started to wonder why I hadn't done anything in my life, yeah I'd had a good laugh but I'd never been to College or University. I had no training or trade behind me and I decided I needed to do something with my life. I decided to become a prostitute. Initially, I thought I could do this for life and live a rich lifestyle but read on. We had an area nearby called `The Dunes`, it was on the seafront and guys cruised there for sex and rent boys. Simon wasn't working much as he was looking after me, we didn't have much money. I was quite excited about the new career. We went down to the Dunes and we walked around in the darker areas. Simon stood at the top to keep an eye on me, I don't know why Simon didn't take the job, he was more attractive than me. Anyway I paraded up and down, bending over to fasten my shoe laces, flaunting my stuff. Everything was going well until I saw this beetle, it was big, black and flying low to the ground and then I saw another. I could see loads of them all around me, I jumped up and screamed like a five year old. My arms a flair, I ran screaming up towards Simon. I don't know what the queens thought but I left dirt in their pubes as I ran past them wailing like a man possessed. Poor Simon thought i'd been attacked. I told him what I had seen and we decided to go home, he was laughing and I was checking behind to make sure the critters weren't following me. The following night I trimmed my body hair, had a long bath and spruced myself up. Simon did the same and we decided it would be safer and more appealing if we offered each other, you know 2 for 1.

We did get the interest of a guy in an Escort. He drove past, we posed, he drove back, we posed, this went on for about an hour or so, we got fed up and walked back into the dunes. There is an underground man made cave down on the front and men often went inside for obvious reasons. We went inside; it was pitch black, 18ft x 22ft. We stood in a corner and Simon lit a fag. This guy started coming over slowly, like a cat burglar sneaking around the edge. I was trying to catch some light to see what he looked like. He was inches away from me and my heart was pounding. I heard him pull down his zip, he put his hand on the front of my jeans and I flinched a little but Simon was urging me on. I moved closer to grab his dick and as I did he said "What the fuck are you doing? I'm trying to have a piss! We can play when I have finished", he whispered. We were both disgusted and all most sick with fear. We went to the pub, laughed, celebrated our failure and got pissed. I might add, I did wash my hands.

Having failed in our first business venture and spent what money we had on getting pissed that night, the next day we decided to find real jobs. We went looking around the shop windows, one advertisement wanted a chamber maid. Simon rang the number, got an appointment and he got the job. I found a job in a Jewish home, cleaning and serving food. I spent a lot of time with a lovely lady called `Rae`, she was 106 years old. The chances are she has passed on now otherwise she would be 120 but I'll tell you what, except for her legs she was a good strong woman and a great character. She used to ask me if i`d sneak in half bottles of Whisky, I'd deliver it to her room and she`d give me the money. The home let her drink but she was only allowed a few bottles a week and she didn`t want the other guests to think she was an alcoholic so I was sworn to secrecy. The truth is she wasn`t, she knew when to stop and sometimes she`d go days without any. The papers came to interview her whilst I was there.

I got her dressed and looking smart and one reporter asked her "What`s the secret to a long life?"
Rae looked at her with a twinkle in her eye, "My secret is a glass of whisky every morning, a glass of whisky every night and the rest of the bottle in between", she looked at me and winked.

I thought `good on you girl`, at 106 yrs old she can do as she pleases.

Although I was enjoying working at the home, I didn`t enjoy the monthly pay. I left to work in a huge block of flats near the Marina. It was about this time that Simon's brother T came to live with us in Brighton. I think he thought it would be great to live in Brighton and being new on the scene, he was looking forward to it. We took him around the local pubs to get him used to the atmosphere. One bar in particular was called `The Bulldog`, there were three steps before you walk straight into the bar area. We persuaded T to go in first and as he got to the top step, I kicked his arse and thrust him through the door. He flew sideways towards the bar and everyone looked at him. In unison, Simon and I said "Welcome to the gay world!" Cruel? No, it was fun and he took it in great spirits. I was still cleaning in the flats. I was assigned to an end wing, where I spent a lot of time talking to a famous tenant, Tony Adams from Crossroads. He was a nice guy, very interesting. He confided in me and told me the truth about things that had been written in the press that year. He was hurt, I could see that. He'd been scorned by a lover for money, blood money.

Chip Pan Alley.

As our apartment was one bedroom we had to find somewhere bigger for all three of us. We found a converted shop a little way out of town but near the hospital, we took it. It was two bedroom and quite quirky, I quite liked it. The shops started from the next door, Dentist, Chippy, Pizza, Indian and then the Super market. T had started working in a hotel a few miles away, I was doing my cleaning and Simon was working at the hotel. Things were quite good, I splashed out on a second hand car, a `Nissan Sylvia` and it cost me £40. We all went out when payday came, sometimes we would eat out or get a takeaway, we considered ourselves `Ten bob millionaires`.

Things started to play up again. I was bleeding and feeling weak again so I went to see the doctor and he arranged a quick appointment. I was right, another blood transfusion. I had a few tests was taken in to a room, and then came the blow. A very nice, wise looking bloke walked in, long moustache, in a suit and softly spoken. He said to me "We have a problem Steve. We've found Cancer cells in the Biopsies and we need to take it out. We have 2 options, we can either take away the Colon and give you a Ileostomy or there's a new operation available. It's called an Ileum internal pouch. We give you a temp Ileostomy for maybe six months and then we'll construct a pouch inside you. You lose the bag and with pills we can control the new bowel." I was in complete shock, I never thought I could die. Simon had terrible nightmares about it but I didn't worry, I just wanted it over and done with. The man was called Mr Farrands, he had pioneered the pouch operation in Britain. Today he's my Hero, I actually spoke with him recently and he still sounds charming.

I decided on the pouch operation. I was 25 and gay, I needed my life and I needed to feel good about myself so I was booked in 4 weeks later. I telephoned my parents to tell them, my Dad, Brother and his family came down for the day. I was unwell and in hospital for another transfusion before the op, I could see the worry on my Dad's face but we had a nice sunny day out. My mum and Pete were quite nearby, they were running a pub in Petworth. The day came and the op was on schedule. I remember Mr Farrands taking the trouble to explain to Simon what would happen, he put both our minds at ease. I woke up groggy and very numb, all was a success but all I could think about was the second op in 6 months. I had a bag on the side of my stomach. The second op to put me back together couldn't come fast enough.

About 2 weeks after the op, it was a Saturday morning and I was boiling an egg when there was a knock at the door. Simon answered it then he walked into the kitchen, all the colour had drained from his face. He told me my Dad was at the door. I thought why would he come down here, then Simon said it, "It's your real dad, birth dad, Melvyn". Years earlier I had paid £7 to the Salvation Army to find my real dad, I never thought I'd meet him. I just wanted to know of him, to see what he was like. I loved Derek, my Dad is an amazing bloke, I certainly didn't want to hurt him but I was intrigued. This bloke was standing in the lounge, dirty looking but clean, like a drunk but smartly dressed. What would you ask your real dad if you'd just met him for the first time? What would be your first words? I said

"Have you got any ID, driving licence or Passport?" but as I said it I saw a ring on his finger. The initials on the ring confirmed it, MLE, Melvyn Leonard Evans. We chatted a little, mainly about me and my recent mishaps and we decided to meet in a bar down the road in twenty minutes. I shot out the door and telephoned my Mother. She was what's commonly known as `gob smacked` and she told me to be careful when we went out. I think she meant for me to see if he wanted anything from me, it was a good job he didn't because I hadn't got anything. We talked about our lives and how he found me, apparently the Sally army had contacted him on Friday and said "Your son Steve has been looking for you, his address is below. Don't go to see him until we have told him your coming, he'll receive our letter on Monday". He ignored the letter and came straight down to see me on that Saturday. We escorted him to the train station late afternoon as he had to go home, we swapped contact details and he left. I wasn't disappointed with meeting Mel, I didn't know what to expect. He was pretty much full on and in your face but then some days, so am I.

Financially we were in the shit, T had found a boyfriend and he moved in with him. Simon lost his job because he got drunk with the hotel porter and I wasn't working for obvious reasons. After a few phone calls Mel asked us to move up to Milton Keynes. We thought about it for about a minute and thought, why not? We drove up to find a house, we saw a great little 2 bedroom semi and so we paid the deposit and took a six month rental. Mel came down to Brighton to help us move. We had Duncan, our lovely Labrador. We had got him a few weeks earlier, he was a rescue dog and his nick name was `table top Duncan` because his back was that wide. Duncan went in the car with Mel, me and Simon went in the Nissan. We were traveling on the M25 when all of a sudden I was hit from behind, Simon swung round to see who it was. He turned back to me and said "It was Mel, your dad!" We pulled over but thankfully there was no real damage, Mel had pulled in behind me.

I said to him "You hit my car, what happened?"
He said "Duncan was in the front seat and he tried to get on my knees. I told him no and stroked his belly, he moved forward and licked my face and that's when I hit you."

You`ve got to laugh haven`t you? I still tell that story.

I still had one more obstacle to confront, the operation. Don`t worry i`m not going to bang on about it but it is part of my life, in fact it saved my life so it needs to be addressed. The house was great, Bletchley was great. Duncan our dog loved the fields; I only had one real problem, Mel! We would open our bedroom curtains at 7.30/8 am and he`d be sat in his car outside, smiling up at us. We would have a coffee and then he`d want to go somewhere. This happened every day and on Sundays he would be outside at 6am expecting to go to a car boot sale. I had another brief encounter with a new business venture, this time a mobile breakfast van. It lasted about two weeks or so. The trouble is I love bacon so as you can imagine, I ate more than I sold.

The time had come, I had to go to Brighton for the op. Simon had to book a hotel down there so Mel had offered to watch our dog. We went south with a kind of anxiety, we knew it was only for a short while but this place had been bad luck for us. We went through the usual booking in process. I had changed my surname again, this time to my real birth name, Evans. We were sat waiting for a Nurse to do blood pressure tests and this 6ft queen came running down to us. "Mr Evens, Mr Evens, I'm sorry I've kept you waiting." He could not pronounce my name, bless him. The op was done and I woke up, this time it felt strange. I'd got used to the bag, I'd become comfortable with it. Now I was re-plumbed and awake with a tube up my rear end, it was bloody painful. Simon visited everyday for a week, he also went clubbing every night and he told me so. After seven days the pain was bad, I was really sore, not from the scar but the tube. Repeatedly I asked them to take it out and repeatedly they ignored me. I am not good with hospitals; I can just about cope with one night. When Simon came in on the 8th day I told him to get my stuff, his own and put it in the car. "We're going home, I'm going to sign myself out" I said. I asked a nurse for the relevant form and she kept stalling so I wrote a letter to the surgeon and waited for Simon. As soon as he arrived I put the note on the pillow and I walked out. I drove from Brighton to Milton Keynes with a tube up my backside and a bag on the end of it. The letter to the surgeon thanked him for what he had done but I also told him to explain things properly to the next patient, especially if they are young like me. I told him the nurses and the care was fantastic but they should listen to patients' grievances more. Oh, and that the food was shit.

It was great to be home, I went into the kitchen and took the needle out of my arm. I went upstairs and laid a mirror on the floor. I squatted over it with a pair of nail scissors and I cut the two stitches holding the pipe in place. I then started to remove it and I soon realised it was up my whistle and as far up as my stomach, it was designed to allow the new bowel to heal. As I was pulling it out, I could feel my stomach pulling also but I couldn't turn back so I pulled it out with a deep breath. It was about 2ft inside of me. I had a coffee to relax, the pipe and bag was in a bin liner near the outside bin. We were just relaxing when a big police van pulled up outside, they knocked at our door. Simon let them in. Apparently they had had a phone call from Brighton hospital to say I had stolen some of their property. Knowing I hadn't nicked their towels, I was stuck to think what they were accusing me of and then it clicked.

"If you mean the pipe and the shit bag in the back garden, it's yours!", I told the coppers.
They looked at me appalled, "Do you mean you've taken it out and you're alright?" one cop said.
"Yeah I'm fine, don't worry" I told them, "I'll go to see my doctor tomorrow".
Within hours I was feeling woozy, I had a real bad time getting used to the new bowel. I constantly felt like I needed to go to the toilet and when I did, I didn't need to go. I got used to it and fifteen years later I still have it. It's the coolest thing I've ever had, it's kept me slim for years.

My little girl, Dixi.

Having had the new plumbing again, my life started to get back on track. The only good thing which happened in Milton Keynes was finding my Dixi. We were driving through Bletchley when a Jack Russell ran under my car, luckily I was stationary at the traffic lights. Simon was horrified, she could have easily been killed. The door opened and he was off, frantically clapping at chickens trying to catch her. He eventually caught her, he had to corner her in a gent's public convenience. She was in a cubicle where she had made a bed. We took her home and soon discovered that she was pregnant, the Vet confirmed it. Unfortunately the pups were too big for her and she lost them all except one, which survived only a few hours. We had her spayed at the same time. That dog went through the best and the worst with me over 19 years. She became my soul mate, I still miss her and I loved her to bits. My new so called father had an Antiques centre with his partner, it was central to Winslow. We used to go over and have a look around. Mel was so predictable, even though he had zero interest in the place he would always approach the customers and say the same thing, "Just checking on my interests". They would just look at him like he was mad man. It wasn't long before we'd had enough and we decided to look around the area. As it was, we were visiting Leamington Spa, Simon's Grandparents lived there. We spotted a nice little place on Rugby Road so we arranged a viewing, signed up and we moved in within 2 weeks. I never really told Mel about our plans, we just did it and told him on the day. Thinking back, it was naughty of us but I really didn't know how to tell him. If Mel would have had his way, we would have been living next door to him and only let out when he wanted us to go somewhere with him, he was that full on.

The new place was a quaint cottage, one bedroom, with a six foot wall around the front garden. One day I was sunbathing when I could hear a party next door so I decided to investigate and soon found a hole in the fence. Being quite nosey, I looked through. There I could see men, all naked and having a garden party, I couldn't believe my eyes. I recognised one of the guys, he was quite tall and dark but not handsome. We had met him in the street where we parked the car. The next day I saw him again so I approached him and told him what I had seen. "Oh yes", he replied "We are always having naturist parties". He told me his partner was called Stuart, he was American. Stuart was quite small with Jam jar bottom glasses but i'll tell you, he turned out to be a great entertainer. We got to know these neighbours and regularly got pissed with them.

It transpired they had an apartment in Leamington for rent, they asked if we were interested and yet again we moved, to a lovely 2 bedroom apartment which was more like a small terraced house. The apartment was in a block called `Charles Court` and it was listed. We soon arranged a house warming party and our new landlords agreed to come along. We had met a few neighbours and one of them called Doris, (I have changed her name and thought this one suited her) seemed particularly friendly. That night, I stuck a note on her car inviting her to our house warming party. Sixteen years later, she's still my best mate. The party went well. Rob the tall dark Australian was an opera singer and Stuart was an entertainer/singer. Simon's parents also came along. We invited a few friends and of course Doris. I have fond memories of that night, Rob had sang `Ave Maria` which had all the women in tears and the second he had finished, Stuart jumped up and crossing his legs he started to sing `There's no business like show business`. It was so funny and a welcome distraction from our tears. As we got to know Doris, she would regularly come around for `wine and cheese nights`. We would look forward to these nights and normally it coincided with watching the Pride and Prejudice series. Mmm...Mr Darcy in those pants! Neither of us can face `Hock` now, we overdosed on it. On a few occasions we would wait until Friday night when Doris had finished work for the weekend, and as she pulled into the drive we would shout, "Get your case ready, we are going camping in Blackpool tonight". Within the hour we would be on our way. The camping was quite fun, Doris would ask me to park my Mini in front of her tent so no one could get in. I remember her saying "I'll never sleep", two minutes later we could hear her snoring away. On other occasions we would get drunk and cook sausages on our camp fire in the early hours of the morning. They were the best meals and great fun, I miss those days but I couldn't do it now, I like my luxuries too much.

Whilst living in this town, I realised there was something missing. It needed a night club, a gay night club. I knew of the perfect building, I had spotted it in near the town centre. It took a few months of business plans and meeting with a big brewery but finally I had an initial `go ahead`. I wrote to a business man I knew and he happened to own the building I had spotted. We set up a meeting at the property and I went through the whole idea with him, he liked it. A few days later he telephoned me to ask me to meet him at `Smith's` restaurant in town, I was to meet him that Saturday. I got all dressed up and excited for this meal I was going to have. At that time, I had only ever had a few meals in restaurants so for me this was a big deal. When I got there I spotted him sat inside with a pretty looking lady, I waved through the window to catch his attention.

He came outside and told me to jump in his car. I thought he was taking me somewhere else, so I jumped in with gusto. I was trying to get Si`s attention to let him know i`d be back shortly (he was sat in the bar opposite), but he was looking the other way. The business man didn`t start the car. He told me "I`ve thought about your plans for a gay club, I think it will work. I have the money for you, it`s come from America. i`ve changed it over to Sterling for you, do your best, spend it wisely and good luck". He passed me a thick brown envelope. He never asked me for a receipt and he didn`t really know where I lived. He just gave it to me, No one has ever done this to me, trusted me like this. I thanked him `a lot` and went over to the bar where Simon was waiting. I sat down next to him, took out the envelope and poured the money onto the table, it was in 50`s. "What`s that? Si said "Put it away! Bloody hell, how much is there?"
I can never tell you truthfully how much this man gave me. I paid him some back and he gave me some more but it was around 20k.
I slept with the money under my pillow, I didn`t trust anyone and that included Si. The next day we went to Blackpool with Doris, the break was previously planned but with a pocket full of money I was determined to enjoy myself. I tipped generously in the bars, we had food in some of the best places and we got drunk for three days. The time had come for me to fulfill this plan. We were sat in a gay bar in Blackpool working out our plans for coming back home and I was concerned I had over spent. Whilst sat there talking with Doris, it suddenly dawned on me that this man trusted me and the day after, I betrayed him. I got the money out of my bag and we started to count it. I was relieved to find we had only used our own money, I was tipping with my own money and I had been stupid. The money I had been trusted with was all there so I decided there and then that I would use it `wisely`. Little did I know I was entering into battle?

Let the battle commence.

Fighting for the license was the most difficult part of this club, I was battling with frustrated Spinsters (magistrates) and bigots. I had to explain over and over again the reasons why we needed this club and the reasons why Leamington had to show support to their huge gay community but they were having none of it. It was time to play dirty. I recruited the help of an ex chief constable and he had agreed to represent us for a set figure, whether it took one month or twelve. The police were objecting on the grounds that there was already a night club on the street, albeit a straight nightclub. They said they were busy dealing with fighting most weekends and a second club would make things worse. They also declared that their cars had to drive up that street every 15 minutes because of the trouble. We knew this was nonsense and my guy organised a couple of weekend spies to sit up all night and record the police activity on that street. When the results were declared in court, we knew we had won. I did on one occasion have to stop the court hearing. One of the magistrates was being blatantly homophobic and I couldn't take anymore, I told them so in front of forty supporters. When they reconvened, the offending magistrate wasn't there and my supporters all gave a big cheer. I was very proud of myself and the community. The results from our spies did it for us. We proved that in one weekend the police had only driven up the street six times and there had been no trouble. The second weekend they drove up the street seven times with no trouble. Our guy had won our case and `The Village` doors opened.

The interior wasn't great but we did our best with the money we had, even with the money from my friend we still had to be careful. We paid very little out for contractors though as there was me, Simon and his parents, his brothers and their uncle. I did very little `physically` but I was doing all the plans, organising inspections and I had to take a National Licensee course. Simon's uncle was a plumber and he worked for pints rather than cash. I cannot use their names but G&S (Simon's parents) were amazing. `S` wasn't in the best of health but we would often find her in the urinals banging in nails, plastering the walls and decorating. `G` had some great ideas, one of them being the bar. He banned me and Si from the club for two days and when we returned, he unveiled the most elaborate bar, which he had built from scratch. It was certainly a focal point. His best idea was the dance floor, which was pretty standard except he had painted `Mincing boards` across it and varnished the whole thing, it was cool. If I never thanked them I will now, although i`m sure I did numerous times.

My club was unique, it wasn't brilliant but you heard good music and had good company. We would put on food most weekends, a free buffet which always went down a storm. We had a great drag queen called `Stella` working behind the bar, his name was Dave and he was a Mechanic. One night he was doing his drag, the next morning he was fitting a new gear box into G`s Ford Escort, a great guy.

Simon thought the beer was for personal use and he was a thirsty lad. He drank a great deal of our profits away and when we had the Guinness tap fitted, it was heaven for him. I suppose most landlords drink socially but he went over the top. He was screwing around also, he thought I didn`t know but I was regularly told he had been seen shagging someone or somewhere. I didn`t confront him because I couldn`t blame him, he was having more difficulties with my illness than I was.

On our main opening night, Si barred one of the Leamington Royalties. It was a close knit community and we couldn`t really afford to upset anyone, we were on a downward spiral from here on in. After a short period of time, his drinking was heavy, it was stressing me out and I decided to sell up. Another dream had to go and I was fed up of constantly making excuses. On a lighter note, I made some good friends from the club, Gerald, Chris and Mark. Doris spent most weeks drinking in the club, she had a drink called `Cute Fanny`. It wasn`t an original name but it was our nick name. Lifelong friends came in the form of Trevor and Gary, they kept my doors open most nights with their drinking. They supported me from day one and they still miss the great nights we had. Having sold what we could, the club closed. I made contact with the business friend and asked him what I owed him.

He told me "When I gave you the building it was a shell, now it's a club. You owe me nothing!"

I didn't want to stay in Leamington, it was embarrassing to admit failure. My mum had a spare house in Yorkshire she wasn't using so we took it. Within weeks of living there we had found a nice little bungalow more central to our needs so we moved again. The bungalow had only one bedroom and an internal coal shed, coil oil in Yorkshire, this was black with years of storing coal. I soon cleaned this room up, I made a window in the door and plastered the walls. With a carpet, bed, curtains and a few pictures I had turned it from a grubby coal shed into a beautiful little bedroom. Doris used it more than anyone and she loved that little room. Doris used to visit often and before the bedroom was made for her, she used to sleep on a blow up bed. One night we pumped the bed up for her and she got inside & snuggled down. In the middle of the night I woke to the strangest sound, there was this enormous farting noise and a ripping sound. I knocked on the lounge door to see if she was ok, I opened it and couldn't believe my eyes. The seams of the blow up bed had given way, blurry-eyed Doris was on her side and the bed had blown itself into a big oval football. We had a good laugh about it the day after.

Sign me up for another one.

I had felt something was wrong for a few days; I was in danger of becoming an expert. The pain in my stomach was getting worse and I was scared of going back to hospital. I had no choice, the doctor came out to my home and he advised me to go to casualty. In casualty they gave me pain killers and when the pain eased off, they sent me home. It was a Friday night and normally we would go out with my Dad to the local club for a drink and to play Bingo. I tell you, we knew how to live! As I was told to rest, Simon went up as usual and I went to bed. I woke up about 9.30pm in the most horrendous pain, I literally thought 'This is it kid, you are going to die'. I had to lower myself to the floor and crawl on my knees to the lounge, I couldn't get high enough to reach the telephone and there were no mobile phones around at that time. I found a shoe and banged on my wall to my neighbour. Seconds later, Carol my neighbour came round and let herself in, she was quick to phone for an Ambulance and was trying to make me comfortable. She telephoned the club to get hold of Simon; I had just been put into the Ambulance when he turned up. At this point, the pain was too much and I passed out. They fought for my life all the way to the Hospital. They told Simon to get my family together and to come up to the hospital immediately. Bloody drama queens, I survived, (obviously). They had to fully unzip me, sort out the plumbing and zip me back up, third time lucky. My only real memory is of my Aunty June visiting me, she was making me laugh but only on the inside; I was so doped up I couldn't even grin. Bless her, she still makes me laugh today but I show more emotion now.

Whilst I was recovering I watched a lot of TV in the afternoons, a lot of channels showed some of the old movies and TV series. I would watch Tenco, the Carry On movies and Norman Wisdom films. I enjoyed these classics and decided to write to the actors and tell them so. I knew Norman Wisdom lived on the Isle of Man, I knew the Carry On films were made at Pinewood Studios and Tenco...I had no idea. Coincidently, two weeks after the operation we went down to Stratford to visit Simon's parents. Whilst walking around the town centre we called into WH Smiths to look at their videos and music. Whilst we were walking around the store I noticed that Si looked preoccupied. We got to the door and he said to me "Hold the door open for that woman, she's famous." I had no idea but if Simon recognised her then she must have been. I held the door open for her and as she got closer, I realised who it was. I stood there like a wally with the door open but she turned away towards the cashier. It was Stephanie Coles from Tenco.

I can admit now that if I hadn't have met Simon I would have had no knowledge of the Carry Ons, Rambling Sid Rumpole, Jules and Sandy, Round the Horn and Alan Bennett. He collected all the above on videotapes or CD. We used to listen or watch these at night time in bed, yes it was that exciting! We also had a collection of classic books on CD, Les Miserable, Oliver and the entire Dickens. I will always thank Simon and his Dad for introducing me to recordings, which even now give me a great amount of pleasure. I wrote my fan letters to Peter Rogers, the producer to the Carry Ons, to Norman Wisdom via the IOM and I wrote to the BBC to tell Stephanie Coles that I enjoyed Tenco and to say that we nearly met. The first reply I got was a signed photo from Stephanie Coles, it also included a penned postcard. She thanked me and said she didn't remember a mad man in WHS but she'd take my word for it. I was thrilled, first contact. Some weeks later, I got a reply from Peter Rogers thanking me for my letter and telling me he was planning another Carry On film. He also enclosed a photo and invited me to ring him one day. I was thrilled to have corresponded with someone who actually produced these wonderful films.

My third reply was from the great Norman Wisdom, a real British legend. He thanked me for my letter and wished me luck with my health. He also told me I'd got a good positive attitude and he ended the letter by saying `you will do well in life`. I was in awe of this man and he had actually written *me* a letter wishing *me* well. He also sent me a lovely signed photo. What nobody knew at the time was that within a year I would be his driver. Over the next 15years I would become a regular figure in his life and he would become such a great friend to me and my family and friends. You'll have to read on for that story. I wrote to a few more stars I enjoyed watching on TV and got more replies. I wrote back to Norman to thank him for his kind words and what came next was to shock the living daylights out of me. We were watching TV one dark and cold Sunday night, the coal fire was glowing and the phone rang.

Simon picked it up, a voice said "Can I speak to Steve please?" Simon said "Can I ask who's calling?" and the colour drained from his face.

He passed me the phone, with a nervous smile and whispered "It's Norman Wisdom".

I stared at him for a few seconds, I thought he was joking.

"Hi Norman, how are you?" I said, it was all I could manage.

He said "Hi Steve, I'm fine but how are you?"

I told him I was fine.

He said "I was reading your letter and I thought I would give you a ring".

We started chatting for a good ten minutes, he was telling me about the Isle of Man and his house. He thanked me for my letter and he told me to keep writing. He spoke with Simon for a few minutes then Simon handed the phone back to me. Norman said "You know Steve; the Isle of Man is a beautiful place. If you ever decide to visit I want you to call me and come round for a coffee, you'll be most welcome". I couldn't believe it, he was inviting me to call in. That evening, there were frantic phone calls to our parents and a big grin on our faces all night. I wrote and thanked him for his phone call, I know what you're thinking. Bunny Boiler? I was so shocked and excited to have spoken with him, I had to write and say thank you. I received a letter about two weeks later, he had written to confirm that I was welcome to visit him and this time he gave me his address and a telephone number.

Again, a few days later he rang up. "Hello Steve, why don't you come to visit me next month for a day? Bring your mate and we can have a chat, some tea and watch a film."

I readily agreed. He told me to write with a definite date and he preferred it to be a Sunday. The next day we made our plans. It was to be the first time we had ever flown in a plane, the beginning of a lifelong fascination for me. We set a date and this time I phoned Sir Norman Wisdom. I told him the date and he said he could arrange for his Rolls Royce to pick us up, I actually declined! I said we would hire a car and at least we could see some of the island whilst we were there. Thinking back, I didn't want to push my luck or let Sir Norman Wisdom go to any trouble. The date was set for the 21st May 1995. After spending a few weeks bragging in the local club, to friends and to neighbours, the day arrived. We set off early to Liverpool Airport, I was shitting myself. I think Simon was but he knew there was a bar at the airport and that would help. The flight was on time, we had arrived early and chilled in the bar for an hour, soaking up the experience.

A Date With A Dream

Although I was scared and the plane was small (27 seats) I couldn't believe I was looking at the clouds from the other side. I was looking through the window when Simon lent over me to look outside. "Get off," I said to him "You'll tip it over" and for a minute I was serious. The trolley dolly came over with a sweet for everyone, no drinks or meal. The flight was only twenty five minutes long so I just chomped on my sweet. Just as we were landing, I realised the sweet was to stop my ears popping but it was too late. As it happens, the landing was fine and I enjoyed it. We did land a few minutes late and it was a further ten minutes before we got off the plane. We had to collect the hire car and buy a map to find Norman's house. All of this took time so I had no choice but to ring Norman to tell him. Ann answered the phone, she told us not to worry and to take our time as Norman was taking a nap.

We found the house relatively easily, even though it took us a good hour. The island may be small but the traffic is slow with lots of villages and sharp bends. We pulled into the grounds of this Spanish style house, white washed with a double garage and a beautiful flowered garden surrounding the whole house. On the wall was a shiny brass plaque, it read `Ballalaugh`. I found out later that in Manx it means `Home of Laughter`. Simon, being a Horticulturist, was looking at the flowers when I knocked on the big wooden doors. Through the shaded window I saw a monkey run from the lounge and across the reception to open the door.

"Allo" it said, it was Norman.

I've been reviewing this sentence and how to describe Norman for a while but it's the only way I can describe what I saw coming towards the door. He invited us in. Ann told me later that he was practicing that run to the door a few times before we arrived, perfectionist you see `our Norman`.

We were taken through the reception hallway into a huge lounge, on the right hand side were two arm chairs and the TV inside a cabinet. On the left was a beautiful but camp 19th century French couch, three seats and two chairs. To the immediate left was the grand piano with a glass cabinet and a beautiful painting of Norman when he was in Aladdin. Norman sat in one of the chairs with his back to a Victorian cabinet which held silver plates from his time in movies. There was one from the Queen and on the piano was a picture of the Queen with Norman. We were in his presence, this legend comedy

49

hero. Ann looked after us supplying coffee and a homemade cake, she offered us huge pieces and I knew then we were going to be friends. Norman resisted the cake; over time Ann told me she had devised a keeping fit regime, D Day. D Day was diet day, one on one off, no cake or biscuits every other day. Norman was watching us eat the cake and he was pretending to dribble, licking his lips. We did feel guilty but I could never refuse a piece of Victoria sponge.

We chatted for an hour or so and then Norman showed us the house and he explained the memorabilia in his glass cabinet. The lamp used in Aladdin was there, it was made from an ash tray. Everywhere you looked was memorabilia, gifts from the rich and famous and gifts from fans, £1 cars to solid silver servers. It struck me that he appreciated everything around him, he didn`t care about the cost. If it's a gift, it's a gift and he treasured them all. He played the piano for us and later in the afternoon we watched `The London Palladium`, it was Norman and Bruce Forsyth doing a one hour gig in front of Royalty and an audience. It was rather surreal watching SNW on TV and sitting next to the guy, priceless. SNW would laugh and then tell us how that bit was filmed or how they created that stunt, we were fascinated. After signing a few photos we had to say goodbye and we thanked Ann for looking after us. We then thanked Norman for everything he had done for us. He said "You should come back again in a few months". And as you've gathered we did.

The next time we visited was with Simon's parents, they were in complete awe of SNW and he lived up to his name. He was larking around with Simon's mum and telling funny stories about his life, he had us all laughing and on my third visit he had us in tears. Doris came with me for the third visit. She had a broken arm and Norman was larking around doing his walk and teaching her how to fall without damaging any limbs. Later in the afternoon, I filmed him telling us about his childhood memories. If you're a fan you'll know he had a poor and sometimes abusive childhood. Well he got to the part where he was homeless and I looked around to Doris who had tears in her eyes so he swiftly changed the subject to something funny and she was smiling. He then went back to his childhood and she was crying again, we burst out laughing. I remember thinking not only can he control his own emotions but he can also control other people's emotions, that could come in useful.

In 1997 I approached Norman with reference to a charity event I wanted to organize, the money raised would be split between Mencap and Manx Mencap. I had approached `The Ardsley House Hotel` to see if they could provide us with a room and a buffet for 55 people at a discounted price of £150. At that rate, I could sell tickets for £15 and still have a decent donation to Mencap. They agreed and thrown into the deal was their best room on a bed and breakfast basis for Norman's use. The room cost me £25 which was a bit of a bargain. Norman said yes immediately, although the arrangements were quite difficult with Norman's new secretary `L'. Ann had retired or at least decided to take a break, as you will see in the book this happened a few times. We finally decided on a date, the hotel was booked and all the plans coincided with some other work Norman had to do down south the day after. I washed and polished my car and washed and polished myself. Simon was to meet everyone at the hotel and keep them there until we arrived.

I was to meet SNW on the motorway at 12pm. He was coming over that morning on the ferry and driving from Liverpool to Barnsley via the M62; easy! 12pm came and went and after 30 minutes had past I was starting to get worried. Simon kept ringing me wanting to know if he had arrived. It was 1pm and there was still no sign of Norman. I decided to ring his agent Johnny, who told me that if SNW was lost then he would drive straight to his apartment in Epsom. I was getting a bit sweaty but Simon had organised for the buffet to be served early so at least the waiting guests would be busy eating for a while. 1.30pm came and went, still nothing. I telephoned 'L' his secretary, she said "He's got his cards, I wrote them out personally." These cards were reminder cards SNW kept in his inside pocket. She said "If he's lost he will ring me or he may go straight to Epsom." Just as the words were coming out of her mouth I could see his car, the BMW indicated and came up the slip road. I told L not to worry and that he had arrived. He gave me a wave and pulled up, I jumped in beside him.

"You're a bit late" I said, jokingly but relieved.

He looked at me smiling, "I knew I'd gone the wrong way when I saw the signs for the Humber Bridge, I had to turn round and come back."

I just smiled. I quickly called Simon and told him we were on our way, he sounded relieved and drunk but I didn't care. I telephoned Johnny to say we were ok and SNW had arrived, he thanked me. We pulled into the car park of the hotel. Simon, to his credit, had organised for everyone to be outside to welcome Norman and as we pulled up he got a huge cheer. Everyone went back inside and as we entered, everyone clapped Norman as he walked to his table doing his famous `Trip`. People were still eating so we took a minute to eat a few sandwiches. Norman seemed eager to get on with it so he started pulling faces and entertained everyone with his singing and messing around. Everyone politely got in line for autographs and a few photos were taken (included in the ticket). It was worth the 2 hour delay. I was pleased my Dad and Jason (my brother) were there because I knew my Dad was a fan. An hour later we were done and I showed Norman to his room so he could have a power nap. I waited downstairs with the guests and one by one they all left clutching their photos and autographs, it had been successful. Simon looked tired and it was true, he had been drinking but then I did leave him alone with over 50 people and we were nearly 2 hours late.

At about 5pm, I called Norman's room to see if he was up and ready, he was glad to hear from me and was downstairs in a shot. I took him to my home, this day was getting better. There were some friends at my house, Ez, Barbara and their eldest son Sean with his wife Rita. We had a good time, just chatting and drinking tea, for 30 minutes or so. I was keen for Norman to meet my Granddad. My Granddad was in hospital and he was barely conscious, he had been ill for a while. As we were leaving, we bumped into Johnny, who lived on the street. He was an Arthur Daly type of character and I've never seen a man so excited. We set off to the Hospital and Norman was in a naughty mood. We arrived and headed for the main doors of the hospital, Norman was running up behind people and licking their ears. You can imagine their faces until they realised it was him. He even tried scaring people by jumping out from behind the lift door. Even in those early days, I noticed something I've called `SNW syndrome`. Wherever we had been and whenever there were people around, I kept hearing whispers over and over again. "That's Norman Wisdom, look", they would all whisper in excitement. It still amazes me today and it shows that people genuinely love him.

My poor granddad was in a near Coma, he had been ill for a while but we were all hopeful he would pull through. When we got to his room I was glad to see my Aunty Jean and Uncle Alan visiting, they looked completely shocked to see us. The look on Jean's face was priceless. Norman shook my Granddad's hand whilst I took a photo, a photo I now treasure and my Granddad never knew about. We had a few more photos taken and then Norman decided he wanted to walk around the whole ward. As it happens, we had arrived after the evening meal so the patients were drowsy and some were sleeping. Norman woke every single one of them with a kiss or a hand shake and he brought that ward to life. It was getting quite late; it was nearly 9pm when we had finished and I was taking Norman back to the hotel. I asked him if he was hungry. He said "Yeah, I'm starving hungry. Let's go to McDonalds for a cheese burger." So we called into McDonalds near Barnsley. We went inside, Norman asked for the wine menu and then he asked what the young girl serving us recommended. The girl just looked at him, no expression.

I wasn't sure about Norman but I was knackered and after dropping him at his room in the hotel, I was glad to get home; I had arranged to meet SNW again at 9.30am the next morning. I was up early and drove over to the hotel to meet him. We had breakfast albeit Norman passed the majority of his food to my plate. A few guests asked for autographs and then we drove towards the motorway, stopping at the car wash for Norman's BMW to have a quick clean. Quick that is until he was recognised and then he pretended to fall out of the car and stagger into the car wash, the manager was in fits of laughter. We said goodbye at the motorway and I was the happiest man in the world, the last two days had been amazing. I had an amazing friend and it was Norman Wisdom, a great guy.

In the year 2000 NW became SNW, Norman received his knighthood. I rang him to congratulate him, it seems he had known for some time but he had been sworn to secrecy. Simon saw the news on TV and he came in to the bedroom with tears in his eyes. "Norman's got his knighthood" he said. I shot out of bed to look at the news myself. In my head I was thinking, 'Well done Norman, you deserve it' and he did. Prior to this I'd written to the Queen at Buckingham Palace to nominate Norman for a knighthood, I received a nomination form which was an inch thick but I ploughed through it and sent it back to the Palace. In March 2000, I got a letter from the Queen telling me my nomination was included in the decision to Knight Sir Norman and a few days later I got a letter from Downing St, also thanking me. As you can imagine I was thrilled, who wouldn't be? I've still got these letters.

We moved to a newer and bigger bungalow that year. I was doing some work for Oakleaf coaches and Simon was at home. We didn't live here for long but it gave us a few memories, memories which I'll never forget. The first was coming home from shopping and Simon putting the TV on, I was putting the kettle on. Simon's parents rang him to tell him to watch the news so he immediately turned it over. He put the phone down slowly as we stared at a plane flying directly into the world trade centre, and then another. For the rest of the evening we watched this terrible disaster unfold in front of our eyes and of course, the rest of the world. We settled back into our routine, work and play. Simon was making the new house look like a home. We were going out often, mostly to the local club with my Dad. My Mum and Pete had also moved to Barnsley, to a bungalow near ours and thankfully the bitterness had finally gone between my parents. Dad was talking to Mum, they had split but they were friends. My Dad had always told me that `time is a healer` and it seemed to be true. Pete is a chilled out guy and over time he became friends with my Dad. Although I think my Dad got a raw deal, everything seemed to have worked out for the best. One day I came home to find Simon listening to some music. I asked him what it was and he showed me the album, it was `Les Miserable. I instantly fell in love with it and we bought the DVD. I was amazed at these people singing and telling the story. Colm Wilkinson had an amazing voice and Philip Quast blew me away, his voice, passion and music is just inspirational. Another thing I can say Simon introduced me to, a kind of music I would never have normally listened to.

My Granddad died, he had been moved to a nearby hospice and died in his sleep. The family were devastated, he was one of the funniest men I'd ever met. To this day we laugh at some of his antics like when for days he'd keep telling us the neighbour was ignorant, every night she apparently ignored him. Two or three times a week we went to the club. If I was driving I'd drop my Granddad off at his home, watch him go inside and lock the door and then I'd go home. If I wasn't driving, my Dad would take him home in a taxi. One night I said to my Dad we should watch my Granddad and see what he's complaining about. We had an evening out and I drove him home with my Dad. We turned off the radio and opened the windows. As Granddad was heading towards his gate, he said 'Evening' to a tall bush in the neighbour's garden, then 2 seconds later he said "Bloody ignorant swine". Me and my Dad burst out laughing. He had been speaking to the bush for weeks thinking it was his neighbour; no wonder he thought she was ignorant. Another occasion I went round to see him and there were wood chippings on the hearth in front of his coal fire. I asked him what it was.

He said "The neighbours keep complaining that I'm chopping wood early in the morning so I've brought it inside to chop the wood quietly on the rug". There's no answer to that is there? He made me laugh and he was a great character. At his funeral we played a song from `Les Miserable`, the song was called `Bring Him Home` and it was very emotional. I got extremely drunk but managed to entertain everyone that night; I also fell out the taxi. The only person missing from the wake was my Granddad. He loved parties and he would have enjoyed that one.

They say things happens in three's and it was surely true that year. We'd had 9/11, then my Granddad died. I had been listening to my `Les Mis` Cd and I wanted my Mum to hear `Stars` sang by Philip Quast. I took the Cd and drove the mile or so to my Mum's. Like most Yorkshire people, I gave a slight knock and walked straight into the house. My Mum was looking frantic and was smoking heavily.

"What's the matter?" I asked

She said "Your Uncle Tom has fallen from a ladder and he's in hospital, he landed on his head".

Before I could say anything, she said "He's not expected to live, what did you come for anyway?"

I forgot all about the Cd and told her to get her coat and bag and we'd go to the hospital. Pete waited at home, he doesn't like hospitals, truth be known none of us do. When we got there my Aunty Susan and Mick were there, they looked haggard and of course worried. My Aunty Sue isn't a well woman anyway and I could see she was thinking the worst. The nurse told us Uncle Tom was in surgery and that she'd let us know what happens. My mum asked Sue what happened. Sue said "He's bloody dead".

After a few moments, she had calmed down and she told my mum that Tom had been working on a client's roof, repairing their guttering when he slipped and fell head first. He survived in a coma for a few days but the doctor said his brain was dead. The only thing keeping him alive was the machine; we had to consider turning it off. All the family arrived and we gathered around the bed. Now, my family are good for a laugh and we all have a good sense of humour. The Doctor and the Vicar came in and they drew the curtains around the bed. The Vicar started to say a few verses and the machine was turned off. As Tom was slipping away, the Vicar continued but he kept getting the name wrong, the first time it was annoying, then we smirked and the third time we smiled. `Patrick was a good man`, `John was a nice, caring person`, 'Philip was'... he just kept getting it wrong. I'm sure my Uncle Tom was having his last laugh before he passed away.

I received a letter from SNW soon after, he had a gig booked in Manchester and asked if I wanted to drive him. I rang him immediately. "Yeah Norman I'll drive you" I said. Arrangements were made for me to pick him up from Liverpool Airport and this time he was on time. His gig was to sing at an old people's home. When we got there Norman went straight into `Wisdom mode` and entertained the elderly audience, singing, joking with them, making them laugh and getting them to join in. One of the old ladies had fallen asleep, god knows how she didn't wake up but as Norman was doing his thing, the lady's teeth fell out of her mouth and Norman accidently kicked them under the audience chairs.

When we got back in the car and I said to him "Didn't you see the teeth on the floor Norman?"

"No" he said. "They won`t invite us back Steve" he continued.
"Why not? I thought you had done well"
"No" he said "They've given me the chop...pers".
I didn't laugh either. I was taking him back to Liverpool for a late flight back home and we were chatting. I asked him what it was like to work with Hattie Jacques and Jerry Desmonde, he said it was `heaven`. he went on to tell me that Hattie was a beautiful, kind soul. Apparently she brought a big basket of food to the filming every day and every day she had cake of some kind for Norman. He also told me about some of the other beautiful women he worked with, pretty young things. "I never had a bunk up with them, well not all of them", he said with a cheeky smile. He fell asleep in the car. I was driving and looking at him, thinking how lucky I was. Only a few years earlier I was watching his films and loving him but I could never have imagined I'd be alone with him, driving him to some of his gigs. We said goodbye and I watched as Norman joked his way through the security, having them on, dropping his suitcase and tripping over his own feet. I thought to myself `does he ever stop or switch off?`

Things were coming to a head with my relationship, truth be known it had not been easy for a while but neither of us knew how to let go. I wasn't completely happy with my sexuality. Oh I knew I was gay but I still doubted myself. We decided to move back down to Leamington, we had left friends behind but we had kept in touch with most of them and I needed some friends around me. We had friends in Yorkshire but my real friends were down south. It wasn't long until we found the right house and moved back down to Warwickshire. I told the family and they helped us pack but on the day we left, I chickened out of saying goodbye to my Dad. I knew he would be upset and to be honest, I felt like I was deserting him. I rang him as I got on the motorway.

Up In The World

My next job with SNW was to pick him up from Gatwick Airport and take him to his apartment in Epsom. We had 2 gigs, one in Bath and the other in Cheltenham. The confirmation this time came from Johnny, Norman`s agent. I kept the letter because it was quite official and it made me feel like I was part of this show business team. The first gig in Bath was a small theatre, Norman was introduced and he came on stage. He did his usual singing and joking around but at the end he introduced them to a new song called `Falling in Love`. It was about getting married for the first time, then the second and then the third. The song was about 10 minutes long and he had over 20 wives! It was brilliant, the song and his performance. In the hotel that night I asked him about the song. He told me he had adapted a play and re named it `Adam and Evil, he wanted to make it into a film and the song was written for it. He told me he was looking for investment but the big wigs thought he was too old. The day after we drove to the gig in Cheltenham. The gig wasn't great but I thought Norman was too good for it anyway. Norman was great but the audience was ignorant, they were young and drunk. I don`t think they knew him like other people did. I drove him back to Epsom the next day. He told me his career had started in Cheltenham and that he thought the world of this place but I could tell he was disappointed with the previous night.

I had made some new friends in Leamington, Rosie and Colin. They were a bit well to do and they were a good laugh. Rosie had a wedding shop and Colin ran a Limo business. Occasionally, I would drive the Limo for them, normally for weddings or parties. I was always talking about their cars to SNW, Rosie had this beautiful gold Rolls Royce which impressed Norman. Whenever we had time to spare we would call into local garages, it didn`t matter which as we were only looking around. Norman would sit in the cars, talk to the staff and most importantly, we would get free coffee and biscuits. It was on such an occasion when we were sitting in a brand new Jaguar, racing green with leather seats. Norman asked me to get the keys as he wanted to see the display lit up. I did as he asked and the sales man gave us the key, he told us not to start it up. I told Norman not to start it. "No I won`t" he said. He turned the key and started switching things on, pressing buttons and turning on the radio, he pushed down on the cigarette lighter and then opened the glove box, The cigarette lighter popped and flew up, landing down the side of the driver`s seat. Norman pushed his fingers down to get it out and replace it. He looked at me with a worried smirk "I`ve burnt the fucking seat" he said. I looked over, there was a ring the size of a new ten pence, it looked like a punch hole. Quick as a flash we were out of that car, keys handed back and with a promise to return, we left.

Laughing in the car Norman said, "I wouldn't buy that one anyway".

"Why not?" I asked.

Tongue in cheek he replied, "It's got a burn in the seat!"

We both burst out laughing.

My health started to play up again, this time I had a new specialist. He was more concerned about removing my new bowel instead of curing it, whereas I insisted on pills, potions and blood transfusions. I had been told about a new cure called Jectifer which meant deep muscle injections of iron. My god, they killed me. For days I would struggle to walk or drive and I had this every two weeks. I found out that every time I wasn't home, whether in hospital or driving Norman, Simon would go out and he would get wrecked. It didn't particularly bother me but it always seemed to be whilst I was away. I would meet a friend and talk with him about Si, normally over coffee. For the book i`ll call him `MC`. We had been friends since I had the club and he was friends with Simon also. I would talk to him about my relationship and he would tell me how Simon was playing away, I would listen and take it all in.

One day he asked me "Do you think Simon would ever have a full on affair?"

"No", I said, "not him, for all his faults he would never leave me. He sleeps around and drinks a lot and he has a terrible temper but no, he would never `shit` on me".

MC agreed.

I had been driving the Limo for J and C when I saw their Rolls Royce in the garage, J told me it was their baby and she only used it occasionally. I fell in love with it immediately, I've always had a love for the colour gold but on this car, it looked amazing. I was talking to SNW about this on the phone and he suggested that we should borrow it one day. It got me thinking. In July 2000, I got a letter from SNW telling me he was taking a cruise to the Fijords. Three weeks later, I got a letter to say he was back.

The letter said "The views and the scenery were absolutely marvelous Steve, I am now at my flat in Epsom. I'm returning to the Isle of Man on Friday, you are welcome to visit". Needless to say we did and on the 2nd October 2000 we went to see Norman again. We had a lovely day with him, we spent most of the day talking about our lives and how different they were. In the afternoon there was another fan of SNW visiting, he was an old presenter from Top Gear, a nice guy and he was excited to be visiting Norman. We listened as Norman and this guy were talking about cars and what their new cars were going to be. I remember thinking how different their world was, it wasn't my league.

In November I got a letter from Norman telling me he was going on a Caribbean cruise and wishing us a Happy New Year as he would be spending Christmas and the New Year at sea. It was about this time that I started to question my friendship with Norman. Was I just an obsessive fan? Was I clutching at his fame? There's certainly a break in my letters for that year. I did sit and think about my situation with SNW. It's true I didn't want anything from him, in fact I'd have driven him for free. I did receive nice letters from him and he was always generous with memorabilia. One thing is for certain, he enjoyed our company, both me and Simon. It's also true that me and Norman spent a lot more time alone together but I felt Simon had always got a good conversation out of him. In a way we complimented each other, all three of us.

Trouble In Store

On the 14th Jan 2001, Ann retired to Southsea and it felt like the end of an era. Anne has always been kind to me and she was a rock to SNW. I got a letter from SNW telling me this and that he had got himself a new secretary, we will call her `SB`. I did have a bit of a panic on my hands. Anne had always replied to my letters quickly, she had organized my driving with Norman and she welcomed us to Ballalaugh, normally with a big cake. I wondered what the new girl would be like, I soon found out.

In my letter from SNW he wrote "I hope SB will be ok and I hope Ann enjoys her retirement." I wrote to SNW a few days later and I asked him asked him if on my next visit I could bring some DVD covers for him to sign. The reply came 4 months later. There was a distinct note of arrogance in the letter and although it was signed by SNW, I knew he hadn't written it. The letter told me that i`d had enough signatures and I wouldn't be getting anymore. Due to the fact I had driven SNW for free most of the time and on occasion I never even billed him for the fuel, I wrote back. I was polite, I addressed it to 'SB` and I made sure she knew who I was. I don't have any letters from Norman from May 2001 until Feb 2002, all my letters were ignored.

I got a reply in March because it had been Norman's Birthday, he was 90. The letter states that Norman had been on a cruise for 2 months, I've found out since that he hadn't. It also said they had got back to 600 birthday cards and letters plus normal fan mail. "SB is getting through it but she needs a cruise to relax", it read, again signed by SNW but not his words. Having received masses of letters from him previously, I could see a difference. I telephoned the house, managed to speak with him personally and he invited me to visit in July that year. In May, Norman went to Albania and made a record out there with Tony Hawks. Tony wrote a book called `One Hit Wonder`. In a letter from SNW, he says he travelled with Tim Rice, who apparently wrote the words for the song which got them to number one in Albania. The band was called `Norman Wisdom and the Pitkins`. The week after, I telephoned SNW just for a natter. SB answered the phone and she reluctantly put him on. "Allo mate` he said. He told me he was in Solihull in a fortnight and he asked if we could meet up. He told me to pick a date within that week, we`d get together, I could meet his pals and on the way home, we could call to my house for a coffee. I agreed to write to him with the details. On the 22nd March 2002 (my birthday), I got a letter to say that my letter had been delayed and he hadn't received it until he got back after his visit to the Midlands. The letter then changes from his point of view to SB's point of view. She states "He didn't have time to visit regardless of the plans made". I was furious. She then babbled on about her new apartment, how much work she has and how she should have an assistant. Well Anne had seemed to cope.

She finished the letter with "Good luck with the filming, break a leg". No comment.

The filming she was talking about was `Last of the Summer Wine`. I had met Alan.J.W. Bell a few times, once with Norman. He was a kind soul, very friendly and I would say a great friend to Norman. This is only my opinion I know but they definitely gelled together whilst I was there. I asked AB about LOTSW and how things were shaping up after the death of Bill Owen. He said that the show must go on albeit Bill will be missed a great deal. He went on to say "It wouldn't be hard to fit you in as an extra Steve, if you fancy it?" I couldn't believe my luck, I thanked him. A few weeks later I got a letter from AB telling me he'd found me a part if I was interested. I telephoned to confirm I was. On the morning of the filming, I had to drive up to North Yorkshire. I got there a around 8am on the Tuesday morning. I was to meet them at a Yorkshire pub, a beautiful area in a quaint little village. I sat there and sat there in my car and finally, at about 9am, everyone turned up. In front of me, were some of the people I had admired for the majority of my life. I was in awe of a very tall Frank Thornton, Brian Murphy who I'd enjoyed in George and Mildred, Peter Sallis, Jean Alexander and Jean Fergusson who is amazingly beautiful and elegant. The legendary June Whitfield was also there and later on in the day I nearly fainted as `the` Thora Hird brushed pass me, looking directly up at my face.

She said "Hello sexy, are you the stunt man?"
I said "No" but I couldn't say another word, my knees were knocking.
To be in a room with these people was enough but to be on TV with them was an absolute dream come true. I watched the cast practicing their lines, I watched them filming their scenes and I was amazed at how long it took to film less than ten minutes of the show. AB made sure I was being looked after very well, I got tea and biscuits and at lunch time we had food from a mobile caterer. I was too nervous to eat, I spent a lot of my time watching and admiring. I just about managed to drink a coffee when Brian Murphy came over to say hi. He is a really nice guy, we were talking about George and Mildred and the cult following it had. Brian told me he had been suffering with a banging headache all day and I was pleased to help

him out with some Panadol from my car. Keith Clifford came over for a chat; he borrowed my phone to ring someone. Later on whilst we were having a cuppa, I was on the phone to Simon's mum when Keith grabbed the phone and had a great long conversation with my mother in law.

It was about 4.30pm when I was called into the makeup cabin. The hairdresser had to spray black paint on to my hair to take out some of the red colour I had in there. With a bit of powder on my face, we were off to film my scene. I was shaking from head to foot, it was terrifying. I had to serve a customer and turn back to the till; the customer then slipped on Brian Murphy's pool ball and threw his tray of drinks in the air, landing on his backside covered in beer. I had to swing around, look over the bar and give a shocked expression... simple. My nerves were getting worse because the stuntman was taking his time and practicing his fall, over and over again. I was watching thinking how bloody hard can it be, it's just a fall. Then I remembered my part and how worried I was. The time had come and I did my bit, then we repeated it and in total my part was filmed 9 times. On the first take I spun round to look at the tuntman but instead I looked at AB. He said with a grin on his face, "That was camper than Julian Clary." I assume that the other takes weren't more 'butch' because if you watch it now they used the first take. We finished about 6pm, I was given a copy of the script and a few of the crew thanked me. I left on an absolute high. Simon was to meet me in `Rainbows`, a gay bar in Coventry. When I got there he was surprised to see my hair jet black, I ordered a whisky and told him about my incredible day. The Last Of The Summer Wine Episode is called `The Liar of the Cat Creature`.

Things were going well with my health for a change; I was enjoying my new life, albeit how limited it was. Every other week or so I would go down to Linslade to visit Mel, my birth father. He was always quite jolly, a little over the top but we enjoyed a few days out, shopping and drinking. His partner Russ (shuffling Jew we called him) was constantly working in their Antique shop in Winslow, `Winslow Antiques`. On the few occasions he wasn't working he would come out with us but I always felt uncomfortable. I don't think he meant to leer at us but he did. They bought a forty foot narrow boat and we would meet on the canal in Bletchley. Going out for a spin on the boat was great, very relaxing. I wrote to SNW and told him about my debut TV appearance. He congratulated me and told me a few stories about his time on LOSW, his character was Bill Ingleton. There were a few scenes with SNW driving a red Mini. Norman couldn't drive it very well and he kept stalling it then he left the handbrake off accidentally. I don't know about you but I'm thinking this is SNW all over, it's not accidental, it's Norman Pitkin.

Things had taken a turn for the worse with my relationship with Si, he was drinking heavily and taking anti depressants. We were having an argument that week and Simon blurted out "I've got anti depressants from the doctor and you never even asked me why". Well the truth was, I didn't care. I had suffered physical health problems and the only reason Si was taking pills was because he didn't have the balls to tell me he was bored with the relationship and wanted out. Don't get me wrong, I didn't have the balls to say anything either, truth be known we had known for a number of years. Like a lot of couples, we just continued in the daily routine. Enough was enough, we decided to part but not really part, Simon moved into the spare room. He was still drinking and I'm sure I wasn't easy to live with. I was frustrated ever since SB had come along and I was breaking away from a 13 yr relationship, I felt my time had been wasted. Every week I would meet up with my mate `MC`, he was the one who had asked me if I thought Simon was having an affair. We used to have coffee, chat and slag off our lives or boyfriends. MC seemed to know everyone and everyone seemed to know him, it's fair to say he had been around. One day I was in the café with Doris, I had £300 in my pocket and wanted a new challenge and something to focus on. I had seen a course at the college, it seemed challenging. I asked Doris, "Should I sign up for the hairdressing course or blow it on clothes?" She told me to sign up and so I did. From day one I never regretted signing up to that course and from day one we were cutting hair. Over the course of two years I passed the course but I gained more than a few certificates. I had a whole new set of friends/family, a new social life and new conversation, I loved it.

Life at the house was unbearable, we were constantly arguing because even though we had split, I was still mother goose and wanted to rule the house. If Simon was out I couldn't sleep until he was in, if he was drinking I'd worry he would start an argument. I often fuelled an argument because I didn't know when to shut up and then one day it all changed. Simon had gone to work, I was cleaning the house and on the side was Simon's mobile phone. I looked at his messages (don't lie, you would do the same) and on there were messages, sex messages and loving messages from MC, my 'mate.` It seemed from the messages that they had been seeing each other for a while. It dawned on me that when MC was asking me about whether or not I thought Si was having affairs, he had obviously been testing the water. I threw a complete wobbly, I couldn't believe my best mate had done this. What he was doing with Simon I didn't truly care about, but the friendship I had lost really hurt. I very rarely trusted anyone with my secrets and now I'd been betrayed. I waited for Simon to come home and as soon as he walked through the door I jumped on him, screaming and shouting. I told him to get his stuff and fuck off, he did. I was quite proud of what I'd done. Not the beating because no one should ever fight unless in defense, but I was proud I'd got him out. The next day, I planned my revenge on MC. The shop where MC was working is central to my town, a shoe shop. I knew he had been stealing from there and selling the shoes to his mates so I rang their office and spoke to the owner. I told them my story over a coffee and told them what he was doing. I had great pleasure standing opposite the shop as the owner and the police went in and arrested MC. As he was brought out to the police car he looked over and saw me standing there, I grinned. Revenge is sweet albeit it makes you bitter and twisted. I only have one regret from that episode. As I was now living on my own, I felt `Dixi`, our dog, was his property. I took her to MC's house, tied her to the door and drove away; the minute I drove away I burst into tears. I knew I shouldn't have left her and it broke my heart, until the next day when I met Simon and got her back. I didn't argue or fight, I just took the dog and left. I'm sorry darling Dixi, but you know I loved you, RIP.

I had a gig to do down in Southend, my friends R and R were part of a Laurel and Hardy group. They met up to celebrate their comedy, talk about the guys and raise money for various charities.

Strangely enough, it sounds quite sad doesn't it but their intentions were honorable and the night I was there was definitely memorable. I wasn't really up to traveling all that way but I had to do it because R and R had asked me to come and talk about driving Norman. I was dead excited as I'd been given Norman's Rolls Royce to drive down in to show it off a bit. They couldn't have Norman but they had me and the Roller. I managed to convince Doris to come down with me, she had been to Norman's house with me and she had met him a few times. Truth be known she sat in that Roller like lady muck, nose in the air and waving to passing cars. We arrived and found the venue without any problem so we parked outside and went upstairs. In the room there were about fifty people, R and R were glad to see we had arrived and after a little break they got down to the evening's events. I was introduced as a friend and driver to SNW. The group did a quiz, they had to watch part of the series `Last of the Summer Wine` and answer questions relating to the episode. As you can guess SNW was in the episode. The last question was `Who was the barman in that episode? ` I looked at Doris, Doris looked at me and before we could say anything, R turned to me and said "The barman was Steve". They pointed to me and I had a look of shock horror on my face, I took a bow. Looking worried I turned to Doris and said "I wasn't in that one, it wasn't me."

Doris told me to go with the flow so I did. There was a break halfway through and I went over to see R and R. I told him I wasn't in that episode and he asked me if I was sure! As usual, Mrs. R had brought us some food so we had a munch and a cuppa. They had a few stalls, craft things and cards so me and Doris had a walk around and bought a few bits as we wanted to support their work. As we were walking back to our seat we noticed a drunken bloke staggering into the room, he took a seat in the middle of the group. I looked over at R and he indicated to me it was alright, they knew him. I watched this man with amusement as he was swigging from a big bottle of beer. He pushed a cork into the top as R started the second half of the night's entertainment. About a minute later as R was talking, there was an enormous `POP` and the drunk's beer spurted out from the bottle, a good six foot high and it went all over the other guests. He was frantically trying to at least save some of it by swiftly bringing his lips to the bottle. Well that was it, me and Doris had the giggles. We were trying to look serious but once we'd got the giggles that was it. Just as I was trying to ignore Doris and pulling myself together, I caught sight of this bloke on his knees with the mop, cleaning under the chairs crouched down so no one could see him. I laughed hysterically but tried to keep my lips closed. I looked at Doris, she was already in fits of laughter.

At that very second, R said "And welcome on stage, Steve". Everybody started clapping, so as serious as I could be I got on the stage and sat on the stool. The idea was to answer the questions the audience fired at me. They were pretty standard questions and I managed to get Doris to answer a few. She gave me a look like she was going to chop my bollocks off but she did great. The finale was a toast to Laurel and Hardy and to Norman and his character colleagues. One by one we had to stand up and toast one of the stars. When it came to me, I had to toast Jerry Desmonde, which was nice as Norman thought the world of him. The very last event was everyone standing and singing `Sons of the Desert`. Ray and Rita thanked me and Doris. Calling me onstage, they presented me with the most wonderful framed photo and signed menu. It was a photo I had had taken with SNW some months earlier. They never fail to amaze me, two of the most generous people i've ever met. Everyone waved us goodbye. I drove around the corner, stopped the car and me and Doris had a sudden burst of laughter. We needed to get it out of our system. We had thoroughly enjoyed the night, Ray and Rita were superb, they had thought of everything and they treated us like royalty.

What's Good For The Goose...

Simon was moving to Wales, he had been offered a job down there and within a month he was down there. I drove him; it was a kind of closure. I thought the village was terrible and I cried all the way home, not because I'd left him, but it was where I'd left him, in time I quite liked the village and the Tapas bar was amazing. I only went to visit him a few times, after that we had different lives and partners.

I was single and it was great. My house was spotless, my clothes were ironed, I looked smart, I was losing weight and my social life was amazing. I got myself into a routine of paying bills on a certain date, washing and ironing on a Monday, cleaning the house everyday but cleaning it thoroughly on Sundays. I'd go out to the bars in Coventry or Leicester on Thursdays and Fridays.

Norman was as busy as ever, he was booked into Bedworth Theatre nr Nuneaton and then we had the Leeds gig. I picked Norman and SB up from Epsom in my own car. The Limo was kept near to where I live so it was better to drive down in my car to save on fuel, the limo is quite heavy. We had a coffee at my place and I took them to the Limo. All bags in the boot, we went straight to the hotel. Norman had a little kip and we were off to Bedworth in no time. This was my favourite gig with Norman, it's the last time I saw him on top form. He was great on stage, the first act was Jess Conran. R and R and my old mate C were there, along with Tammy my hairdressing tutor. We surprised Pat and Tony (Tammy's parents) with free tickets and a chance to meet the man himself, I was good at making dreams come true. Norman was brilliant that night, even though I'd heard the show a thousand times he was brilliant, every one was thrilled. All my mates came back stage to see SNW for photos and autographs. SB came up to me, "Steve, there are about fifty people waiting for autographs downstairs, will you tell them all to fuck off?" I just looked at her.

I went downstairs and there were more like a hundred people waiting. I got their attention and explained that Norman was thrilled they'd enjoyed the show but he was heading towards 90 and was very tired. Well, you'd have thought I'd just shit on their heads, there was chaos and people shouting at me. I managed to smuggle Norman into the Limo just as three youths climbed on top and ran the full length of the car roof. A woman was thrusting her number into my hand explaining her mother was dying and she wanted an autograph, I slipped it through the window and Norman signed it. The police were there, they were directing me out of the car park. I had to reverse and a copper was directing me. Bang, I felt it through the car but the cop told me not to worry, it was only a bollard. I wasn't worried about the bang, there were about a hundred people crowding me as I was trying to get SNW and SB out of the area. Finally we broke loose and we were on our way back to the hotel. Norman was knackered and I was knackered so I dropped them at reception and went home, parking the Limo on my drive.

The next day, I took my car as I only had to drive them back to Epsom. It was a nice easy run, thank god! The night before had been quite fun, it was only one night but very exciting. I was looking forward to the next gig in Leeds. It was a four day event starting in Leamington where I lived. Rosie had organized a charity event for orphans in Sierra Leon. We were using their Limo and Rolls Royce to drive SNW around, in return for Norman (at a later date) speaking at a meal they were arranging. I drove the Limo to Birmingham airport to pick up Norman, he was flying over with SB. I rang the airport in advance and they cleared the way for my Limo to park right outside the arrivals, it was great. Security let me through all the cones and whilst I was collecting SNW they had police around the Limo clearing the way. Trevor and Gary, my friends, were following in the car behind to cover my back in case the Limo broke down, I never did trust that car. When Norman came through customs, he made a little run towards me, smacking a big kiss on my cheek and thrusting the suitcase in my hand. "Carry that Steve", he said.

When we got outside there was a group of people waiting around the car to see who the star was. They cheered and clapped at Norman as he did his `walk` to the car, tripping up over the kerb and getting into the back of the car with SB. SB had a face like thunder, I could see she wasn't happy. I asked her if she was ok and she told me SNW had been playing her up all the way over from the Isle of Man. "He won't like this car Steve, if he can't sit in the front he won't like it", she said. Unfortunately she was right; I'd forgotten he always likes to sit in the front. It had been nearly a year since I'd driven him and I should have known better. I told Norman that we would swap the Limo for the Roller later on, I knew he liked the Roller and it seemed to cheer SB up also.

Whilst they freshened up at the Hilton in Coventry, I sat in the bar going through my itinerary. We had to drive to some friends of mine at Bunters in Leamington, it is a sandwich shop and I had promised them I would bring Norman the next time he was in town. Then we had to go to Rosie's wedding shop in Warwick to promote the shop and then off to Leeds for three days. Norman and SB came downstairs to join me. Norman was looking a little thin, I hadn't noticed before when I picked him up but with his jacket off he looked thin. I mentioned it to SB. She smirked and said "We haven't got time to eat have we Normee?" There was something in her eyes I didn't like. We ordered some sandwiches and cake and for two hours we talked about the next few days' events and Norman's career. SB questioned me on how long I'd known Norman, what I done for him in the past and how we met. It took her that year to realize I wasn't just some fan. I had been driving him, I had become friends with him and Norman loved seeing me. I think I was finally getting her onside.

The next day I duly turned up in the Roller, all washed and shining. Norman and SB were in good spirits, we went to see Jan and Craig at Bunters and had a coffee and a bacon sandwich (the best in town). We were about 20 minutes late meeting Rosie at the shop in Warwick, there were a few press there, cameras flashing and a few fans. After maybe an hour we set off to Leeds. All the way up the M1 Norman was chatting with me, SB was dosing in the back. He was telling me about his cars, houses and career and then he started talking about his son, daughter, daughter in law and grandchildren. This was all news to me. I knew he had kids, I often spoke with him about my own but he was telling me all about his. His daughter had been an actress in America for a while, his son was a cricketer and now owns a sports shop and his daughter in law was looking after the family and their children, Nick, Jackie and Kim. I was very interested because our conversation hadn't got to that level in our friendship. Id' known Norman for 8 years and I'd never met them or not knowingly. I did meet Jackie once at Ballalaugh but I couldn't swear on it and of course, I didn't realize who she was.

We were about 15 miles from Leeds when something started to go wrong with the Roller. I could hear a spinning noise, whirling around at high speed and the car was losing power. With my foot down I found I could maintain 50 mph, I kept calm because I thought if I can get him to the hotel at least he's settled until I can sort the car out. We limped into the hotel, I helped them both into reception. In

71

the back of my mind I was hoping resting the car for a few minutes might sort the problem out, no such luck. At reception SB produced a credit card for booking in and the receptionist swiped it.

"I'm sorry but its been declined" she said.

Quick as a flash SB said "Can I at least get SIR Norman to his room and I'll come back down and deal with it."

The receptionist obviously hadn't recognised Norman at first and he looked taken back as he realized. "Yeah, sure", he said and they went upstairs.

I used their directory and phoned a Rolls Royce mechanic to tell him about the car, he said to bring it up immediately. I telephoned Rosie to tell her about the car. She said "No problem, whatever it costs get them to bill me." The car is great, big, bold and beautiful but driving through Leeds at 15 mph with a noise coming from the underneath like a small jet engine, was rather embarrassing to say the least. I limped my way in to the garage. The mechanic told me I was lucky to get there as the petrol motor had burnt out. Whilst the car was in the air I could see what had been making the noise, the petrol pump was whizzing around like a small turbo. He said he could put a new one on but it would be tomorrow, I had no choice but to say ok. I caught the bus back to Leeds and telephoned my parents. They were only 15 miles away in Barnsley so my Mum's husband Pete came to my rescue. My mum and Pete had a brand new little car, Perodua Nippa. I'm not sure which country it comes from but for a 850 engine, it could fly up and down the motorways. Pete came to pick me up, I dropped him back home and went back to the hotel.

I decided I'd had a long day and went to the reception to get my keys.

"You're not booked in here" she said.

"What? I'm the driver to SNW, he's upstairs and he's due in theatre tonight. I need to catch a shower and get dressed for driving him" I replied.

If I am driving SNW to an official gig I always dressed smartly in a suit, the chauffeur bit you see. On a casual drive or visiting him, I always wore a shirt and tie but normally with some nice jeans. I telephoned my mum and arranged to sleep there. I wasn't really worried that SB hadn't booked my room properly, I wasn't going to bother them as my parents were nearby and I knew SNW had a busy few days. I freshened up in the hotel toilet and got down to my pants in the car park, emerging like Superman but with my suit on. Now the Perodua was small, which was fine as me and SNW are both short guys but SB was quite tall and as Norman liked to be in the front, she was squashed in the back.

The grand theatre is a beautiful theatre in the centre of Leeds, Norman was playing two nights. That first night went really well, Jess Conran was on with SNW. They were great friends and helping Norman out with his memories (as a backup) on stage was Keith Simmons. The show went really well. A woman at the back of the audience was shouting 'Norman' all the way through. The poor woman was dying of Cancer, she had been in hospital when Norman was playing Bedworth theatre. The family had written to SNW to tell him this and he arranged to pay for a taxi from Bedworth to Leeds and back so that she could see the show. We met her later in the evening backstage; they thanked Norman with a box of chocolates and some flowers for SB which was nice. Backstage there were friends of Norman's, a few fans and the staff. One of the members of staff cornered me, "There's a couple of fans at the back door waiting to meet Norman." I had a quick word with SB and I took Norman to the stage door. As he was signing I jogged back to grab his jacket as it was cold, when I heard SB talking to Keith and Jess.

"He thinks he's his fucking bodyguard, I've got to get rid of him" she said.

I popped my head round so she could see me and just raised my eyebrows, she caught sight of me and smiled, embarrassed.

That evening we went back to the hotel and I dropped them off. Inside I was fuming but I bit my tongue and said goodnight to Norman, assuring him I'd take him out for a drive the next day. I slept at my Mum's that night, paranoid at what SB might be saying to SNW, I didn't sleep a wink. I needn't have worried, the next day Pete took me to collect the Roller and we were back in business. I got to the hotel early with the intention of having a quick cigarette before we set off. I telephoned to say I'd arrived, Norman answered.

"Hi Norman, I'm in the car park, I've got the Rolls Royce back," I said.

"Oh great Steve, I'm coming" he said.

Quick as a flash he was in the car park, running over to me like only Norman Wisdom can. I asked him where SB was.

He said "She's a c**t Steve, fucking c**t."

At that moment she came walking out, all smiles.

"I'm going to have a look around Leeds Steve, you take him out and get him back for about three so he can have a nap before tonight" she said, swinging round and walking back through the doors.

I was thrilled to bits, most of the day with just me and Whizzy. We drove into the Moors, just cruising along. We called in to thank the mechanic who had fixed the Roller and then we drove over to Wakefield Garden Centre Cafe for a coffee and a bun.

"Well Norman, what do you fancy doing?" I asked.

He took a big mouthful of his Victoria sponge and spitting crumbs everywhere he said "Let's look at cars". So we did. I rang round a few places and found a Jaguar garage and next door was Chrysler. I telephoned to say we were coming and within twenty minutes we had arrived.

The Jaguar garage was great, Norman was like a child in a sweet shop, running from car to car, sitting in them and pressing buttons. The staff were in awe of him and he knew it. After a few autographs and photos we went next door to the Chrysler garage, where Norman spent nearly an hour inside one of their cars, chatting with the sales team and test driving the car in the car park. I think they thought they had a sale but they hadn't.

As we were leaving Norman said "Lets just go back and look at the Jags again".

So we went back and after another 20 minutes or so the sales guy came over to Norman.

"So do you want to buy it Norman?"

Norman asked "Have you got it in racing green?"

The guy said yes, Norman turned to me and winked.

"How much is it?" Norman said.

"£27000" the guy replied.

"For cash?"

"Ah, for cash you can have it for £21000, Norman" the sales guy said.

Norman said "I'll bring £18000" and a few months later he had it.

It was getting late now, it was past 3 and I didn't want to aggravate SB, so I told him we had better make a move. We got in the Roller and the snow started, by the time we had got back to the hotel it was snowing heavily. I took him inside, it was about 4.30pm but I didn't care. As I went to use the reception phone to ring SB, I noticed her slumped over the bar, she looked like she'd been drinking there all day. I took Norman to his room and told him to have a rest, he thanked me for a great day. I bought a coffee in reception and sat behind SB, as she was coming around I said hello, she jumped a mile.

Pulling her hair back into shape and glaring at me she asked, "What time did you get back?"

"About two hours ago, Norman's asleep upstairs", I lied.

She came to sit with me and there was something in her eyes, sadness. I asked her if she was ok and she said yeah, she thanked me and went upstairs.

I sat in reception until about 8pm and freshened myself up, by which time they were both dressed and in the Rolls Royce.

SB said to me "Don't suppose you can do me a favour Steve? A friend of mine is nearby and he needs a lift tonight. Would you mind picking him up with his wife and bringing them straight to the theatre?"

"Yeah sure", I said. "Who is it and where?"

She gave me the address, it was Tony Hadley, the footballer. Pete was thrilled when I told him. I found the address and through the snow blizzard and hail stones as big as conkers, I got them to the theatre. SB was thrilled and said she owed me one, I thought too fucking right you do. The show was great again and afterwards we went to find a restaurant but we couldn't find one so we ended up with a takeaway in the hotel. SB said to Tony `Why don't you stay the night? I will put it on Johnny Man's card." Tony agreed. That night she had a few more drinks then she got up, caused a scene with SNW and stormed off to bed. Keith went after her and I sat with the rest. Ten minutes later she came down with red eyes and sat next to me.

"Are you alright?" I asked.

"Oh yeah Steve, it's just the things you do for love and when there's no love, what can you do?"

To this day I've got no idea what she was talking about but I left them to it. It was about 2am and as I didn't have a hotel room and it was too late to wake up my parents, I drove the Roller into Leeds City Centre and went to a Gay night club. I got loads of attention in my suit but I wasn't really out to pull, which was lucky because I didn't. I drove the car to the M1 Services near Barnsley and I slept in the car. I woke about 8am, I'd only had a couple of hours sleep but I felt ok. I freshened up in the services, had a coffee and went back to the hotel.

Today we had very little to do except a BBC interview and driving Norman and SB back to Epsom. The interview was at 5pm so we had a whole day to kill. We went shopping and ended up in Harry Ramsden's for Lunch. SB told me Johnny would pay on his card so we could have what we wanted. Well, I'm allergic to fish so it was chips and sausage for me. Norman went the full hog and ate it all, to my surprise. SB started chatting again, she asked me about SNW`s kids, whether I'd met them and what they were like. I told her I hadn't met them, I don't know why but our paths hadn't crossed. She seemed to want to know how big a part they had to play in his life, to which I couldn't answer. After finding Norman sat on another table with a young family, she indicated for him to come back and join us, I seized my chance.

"Norman, as we have some time to spare after the BBC interview, do you mind if we call in for a minute to see my Dad and then around the corner to see my Mum and Pete? It wont delay us and we`re in plenty of time", I said.

Norman readily agreed but SB said "I don't think we can do it, I don't want him tired".

Norman said "Yeah Steve, of course we can".

I turned to SB before she could say anything and I said "Come on S, you owe me one remember? I picked up the footballer."

She said yes. At the BBC Norman was due to be interviewed on the local news. I was in the green room telling my mum we were going to call in and Norman grabbed the phone.

"Allo Sylvia, will you get some crumpets and jam in and some cakes please?"

My mum said she would. I telephoned my Dad to say we were calling in. My mum said it was strange because one minute she was talking to SNW, the next minute he was live on the BBC news.

We got to my Dad's house and spent a good fifteen minutes with him, Norman noticed a photo on the mantelpiece. He was quite surprised by it because the photo was of my Dad, my brother Jason and Norman in the middle, they had met at the first charity gig I did. I remember wondering how many people have met SNW, probably had a conversation with him and a photo with him. It is impossible for Norman to remember them all, even though these people cherish the memories. We left Dad's and went to see my mum and Pete. Norman had a bunch of flowers in his hand for my mum.

SB said "Oh Steve, Norman doesn't like giving women flowers, he doesn't want them to get the wrong impression."

Norman looked at her and said "Nonsense, it's Steve`s mum."

With that, he ran off down the path and with a voice that would wake the dead, he shouted "SYLVIA" as he knocked on the door. I did smirk a little; my mum had got the best china tea service out, serving Norman and SB with everything he had requested. There was Victoria sponge and fresh cream cakes on the table. What we hadn't realized was that as Norman was in Yorkshire in theatre, the local Yorkshire television was playing his films and Norman noticed it on TV. That was it, we were stuck watching a wisdom film with Norman himself, scoffing cakes. He had 4 cream cakes and a piece of Victoria sponge after the crumpets. Needless to say, he was content and fell asleep in the chair. Mum's neighbour came round to meet him and as we were leaving all the neighbours were hiding behind the net curtains trying to get a glimpse of SNW. We took some great photos outside the house, my mum, Norman and Pete in front of the Roller. I had a long journey ahead of me, Barnsley to Epsom. We were already late and by the time we arrived at Norman's flat it was gone 10pm. Just as I'd parked up SB told us she'd lost the keys, so Norman had to wake up an unimpressed neighbour who had a spare set of keys. Once we were inside, it was down to the dirty business of money. SB had worked out my salary for the few days and it was

£860, not bad I thought. She said she would get Johnny to send a cheque but I never got it. I did have a last bit of fun though, the Roller and me on an empty motorway. The next day Norman rang to thank me for a great few days and he asked me if I'd like to drive him again in a couple of weeks.

"Yeah, go on then," I said.

Walking Happy

Life went back to normal for a while. I had been making plans at college; I quite fancied the idea of doing a fashion show and donating the proceeds to Cancer Research so I started to put my ideas on paper and enquired within the college to see how they could support me. Fellow students at the college were very supportive and between them all we came up with an idea, a venue and a show. W decided to also have an auction, I put a letter together and sent it direct to the homes of a few famous names I had come across. It wasn't long before I started to receive replies or should I say parcels. Victoria Wood was very kind, she literally gave me the coat off her back, a signed leather jacket. On a visit to Pinewood Studios, I got to meet a very beautiful guy called Johnny Depp, you might have heard of him. He was filming Charlie and the Chocolate Factory and after a brief chat he signed a `Pinewood` tee shirt for me. Stanley Baxter sent a very rare annual/autobiographical, Gary Linneker sent me a Match of the Day signed script along with a signed photo and letter wishing us luck. Roy Barraclough sent a tie which he had worn in Coronation St along with a signed photo. I suppose the best item I received was from Julian Clary. He sent me a John Paul Gautier black sparkly top he had worn on Strictly Come Dancing, it cost 2k. I included a signed letter from Charlie Kray and a few SNW items. We had also decided we could sell some of the clothes in the show. I knew how to plan this fashion show but I needed someone with flair, someone who was radical with their fashion ideas. A few weeks earlier I was at the local hospital, we were early for visiting so we were having a coffee in the canteen. Through the window I saw something I've never seen before. This lad was walking (mincing) down the corridor in what I can only describe as `Fred Flintstone` trousers made of fur and a black skin tight netted top. This guy wasn't slim, he had big goth boots on and a handbag shaped like a Heinz tin of beans. His hair was blonde and pink and punky, I couldn't take my eyes off him.

A few days later, I was in a café in Leamington with Trevor when this lad walked past the window. I'd already told Trevor about him and there he was again, I decided to risk it. I told Trevor to wait for me and I ran out after this guy. He looked a little startled as I ran up behind him and tapped his shoulder.

"Hi", I said. "I am Steve, I'm planning a fashion show and I've been looking around for inspiration. I wouldn't mind your input."

"Hi Babes" he said. "I could help you, I'm Darran. Meet me in the 02 bar on Sunday and we'll chat".

I thanked him, swapped numbers and went back to the café. That Sunday I went to the bar, it was a gay night so there were a few guys in I knew but no sign of Darran. It was getting late and I was losing the stamina when all these people started to crowd this guy in a full length cow print coat. I found out afterwards that he'd made it himself. We had a good long chat, recruited a couple of the boys for models and Darran agreed he would come round to my house the following night in a taxi. He said he would bring a few bits he had but I wasn't prepared for the taxi turning up with three suitcases of makeup, wigs, hats, dresses, jewellery and handbags. Oh my god, the handbags! Every design possible, shaped like Stilettos, hats and the infamous Baked Bean bag. There was everything and more and by the time the evening was ending, we had got together some 30 outfits with inter changeable accessories. I needed a venue but it was difficult as I also needed a forty foot catwalk. My local bar at that time was the 'Moorings', situated on the Grand Union Canal. As a bit of a thank you, I invited Darran and his partner Daniel to the Moorings for a meal. After I had paid the bill we were walking downstairs to the bar area when all of a sudden I felt like Kate Moss. I had just walked down a spectacular staircase and in front of me and the bar was a forty foot wooden walkway. All dark wood with a fitted carpet surrounding it; it was perfect and exactly what I had been looking for. It was in front of my nose all this time. I had a word with the manager and he agreed we could use it.

My colleagues from college all gave up their Sunday mornings and every week we met at the bar to practice the walk and the moves. To make some extra money, I thought we could have a buffet downstairs. We added £3 to the ticket and offered a meal for two including Champagne and four courses for £40. The management struck a deal with me and we got all the food for 50% of its cost. One of my tutors had a husband in a band, they agreed to play for us between the fashion shows. There was to be 4 fashion shows, Punky, Gothic, 80`s and the final was a mixture of fashions. They were all Darran's designs including a beautiful wedding dress (donated by Rosie), which was used in the Gothic and punk show. Selling tickets was easy because of the venue and staff, my colleagues at college and a small advertisement. We sold out in no time and the pressure was on to do this professionally. I only had one more thing to sort out, I needed an auctioneer. My friends would have me tell you about the day I accidentally gave a BJ to a very famous Antiques expert. I was feeling at little frisky, I really wasn't bothered about going to a bar to pull and I'd been told about these woods where men and women went for sex. I thought I'd try it out and within minutes of walking into the trees, I noticed a shadowy figure approaching me. We didn't say a word and before long I was getting a Blow Job. I returned the favour to this guy and we walked back to our cars. As we approached the light I looked at this guy (to see if he was a minger) and I had the shock of my life, he was from TV, an Antiques expert. I smirked a little, duly said `thanks' and got back in the car.

A few weeks later, I was having a clock valued for auction and it was the same guy, he started to tell me all about the clock and what it was worth.

As I thanked him he said in a low voice "Where do people like you go for a drink? Is there anywhere in Leamington?"
I just smirked again and told him, "People like me and you go to so and so woods."
At that moment he recognized me, he went very pale as I was leaving. I wrote to this guy to ask him if he could help with the fashion show, unfortunately I reminded him who I was, needless to say I never got a reply. I also approached Tracy Dawson, Les Dawson's wife. I had been in touch with her since Les`s death, they have a beautiful daughter

called Charlotte. She agreed to come down along with the Roly Poly's but things went wrong, the post went missing. The night before the gig they telephoned me to say they couldn't make it, which was a shame because Mo Roland is such a great woman and game for a laugh, I was hoping to get her on the catwalk. I was beginning to despair when I remembered an auctioneer who lived relatively close to our town, his name is David something. I decided to write to his office and immediately I got a reply from his secretary to say that he would love to do it. I sent them my itinerary and he confirmed. That was it; I had the frocks, the models, the venue, the audience, the experts in hair and beauty and finally an Auctioneer.

The day arrived, 21st March, the day before my birthday. Alex, Cindy, Mike, Betty, Claire, Jo, Sarah (all colleagues from college), Lucinda, Darran, Big Paul, Trevor and Gary, 12 models and staff; they all gave up months to help me and I thank them all. The show was an absolute success. Ray and Rita set up a stall to sell cards, the styling, makeup and clothes looked superb, the weeks of practicing the catwalk was faultless. After the first two parades, we had the buffet, my parents had their meal with David the auctioneer. The band played throughout the interval. The second half of the show went just as well, Alex did four costume changes in 30 minutes, complete transformations albeit he had the body and looks. Claire wore the wedding dress in a punk style and the finale was Darran with the same wedding dress but 'gothed up'. It was a fitting end to the parades. David performed a great auction, getting hold of every penny he could from the audience. We raised over £1000 for Cancer Research, I was very proud. My speech at the end was very emotional, drunken emotions (it was my birthday)! I thanked everybody including my friends for putting up with me. My top two auction bids were for the Victoria Wood signed jacket which raised £140 and £170 was raised for the Pinewood studios Teeshirt signed by Johnny Depp. I dedicated the show to my Aunty Pam who had just battled with breast cancer.

Steven Evans

Just My Luck

Some of you are probably wondering why I never involved Norman. Well for one thing it wasn't his scene and the second, I was being ignored. SB had stopped all contact. I was getting increasingly worried about SNW, he was never available when I called and my letters went un-answered. I kept trying but SB kept telling me he was sleeping or on holiday. In November 2004 I decided to ring again, this time SNW answered, he was pleased to speak with me. Within minutes he had invited me over in February for his 90th birthday. He asked me to hold on and he went to get his diary to make a note of it. All the time I was expecting SB to come to the phone but she didn't. After a good old catch up we said goodbye. I followed up the plans with a letter, within days I had SB on the phone.

"How dare you make plans behind my back? How dare you speak to SNW whilst I'm not there?" she was swearing and screaming down the phone.

Obviously she wasn't happy but I didn't care.

I told her "Look SB, you work for SNW but you are not his wife. He has his own mind and I am coming on that day with 2 friends, I've cleared it with Norman so you can expect me."

She slammed the phone down. I didn't tell R&R as I didn't want them worrying. I followed up the plans by letter again. At first she kept writing little notes stating they won`t be there as he was filming but I kept writing back as if I hadn't received anything from SB. Finally SB rang me, the day before I was going. "What time are you coming Steve? I just wondered if you can pick a few things up from the UK and maybe post some mail in the UK for me when you go back?" I told her I would post his mail but I couldn't bring anything as I had my own luggage. Surprisingly she was really nice, telling me not to worry about it.

I met R&R at the airport, it was a big day for Ray as he hadn't flown since 9/11. When the 16 seater plane pulled up it didn't help but he was fine, I think it was a little cramped for him. It put me off when I saw the pilot taking suitcases and putting them in the tail of the plane. I remember thinking ` I wonder if he knew he'd be handling luggage when he made the decision to be a pilot`. The best was soon to come though. When we were all aboard and there was only a curtain between the pilot and us, he whipped it back with a cheeky grin on his face and said "Enjoy your ride, I'm expecting a nice easy flight. I don't need to do the drill do I? We all know what will happen if we go down!" With that he closed the curtains and we were off. I looked at R&R and they looked worried. What they didn't know was that this plane was the smallest I had ever flown on and I was shitting myself. We arrived no problem and got our hire car to travel the hour or so to Ballalaugh. The Isle Of Man is small and you would think a person could drive around it three times in one hour but it is quite a slow island. The traffic is calm and the villages are so small, you have no choice but to drive slowly. God knows how they cope in the TT races.

To say there was tension when we arrived is an understatement, you could cut the atmosphere with a knife. I got the impression that SNW and SB had been arguing and I could see by her face that she had been drinking. I bit my tongue and went to sit with Norman. I could see he didn't look well, in fact he looked thin, I held his hand and stroked it. I don't know why but it's something I did, I stroked these old hands. Norman didn't seem to mind and we caught up on a bit of gossip. R&R were pleased to see SNW, they had baked him a cake and covered it in Licorice allsorts, it looked tacky but I understood their idea and these were Norman's favourite sweeties. The intention was nice and Norman thought it looked nice, SB was in the kitchen the whole time. I took the cake through to have it sliced and she jumped a mile when I walked in the kitchen. She was just polishing off a glass of something when she said "What's that?!" with a big grin on her face. I told her it was a gift from R&R and she burst out laughing loudly, almost choking herself. The cake was funny but not that funny so I just stared at her. She got the message but as she was passing me a plate and knife she was grinning like a Cheshire cat. I felt a little uncomfortable as I walked back to the lounge, I could see the hurt on Rita's face, she had obviously heard SB laughing.

We had a cup of tea and some cake and talked with Norman. R&R had made a beautiful red double decker bus advertising all of Norman's films, they use it for donations in their shop. If I'm repeating myself then I'm sorry but Rita makes amazing cards for birthdays and weddings and she sells them for donations to Manx Mencap. Anyway, they wanted a photo of Norman and the bus but it didn't work, Norman liked it and they ended up giving it to him. Bugger always gets his own way but how can you say no? They couldn't and neither could I. I had a chat with SB in the kitchen before we left. I explained to her that I want nothing from Norman or herself, the driving is great and I always look forward to seeing SNW. I was building up to an argument but she apologised and told me that loads of his fans and friends want him for his money. She realized I didn't and said not to lose touch because he needs his friends. We left on good terms, or so I thought. Three weeks later I did a series of driving assignments, from his flat in Epsom to London, Southsea and Brighton. All were great but I did notice SNW was getting old, looking unwell.

My own health wasn't great, I was having bouts of stomach problems. I soon realized that the pouch inside me needed attention now and then, medication or blood transfusions. To date I've had over 110 transfusions, they are very effective but long winded. I was having on average 3 units of blood, which took 4 hours per unit. Inevitably this meant an overnight stay and I hated it. I had a reputation for walking out, signing the necessary forms or just pulling the needle out to leave immediately. I discovered if I tweaked the line control on the transfusion tube I could speed the procedure up. On a few occasions I speeded it up too fast and went a little dizzy and sometimes, quite high, it was great. My internal pouch also has a tendency to block or become narrow, this causes light pains which progressively get worse until I can't cope anymore. Most of the time this results in a further unzip and investigation. I can only describe it like giving birth and ladies trust me, I'm sure it's very similar. I can endure an enormous amount of pain before I will accept drugs. I was offered a new kind of treatment to stop the transfusions, it was a deep muscle injection into my thigh, also used for pregnant women. It was called `Jectifer` and my god it killed me. Thankfully, after 2 years these were stopped, not suitable apparently.

I got a letter through the letter box, it was from SB. She asked me whether I would like to drive SNW to a gig in London, it was a three course meal with other stars at the Grovenor Hotel. I rang her to accept. "Put your best suit on" she told me, "it's a posh do and you will be eating with us". When the day arrived I got dressed in my black suit, looking quite dapper and I drove to Epsom. Norman was pleased to see me and he was dressed accordingly, even SB had made an effort. We drove slowly through the rain and slush and in London we drove through snow. We parked at the rear, there were press taking photos as SNW arrived, we took our seats. I looked around me, there were famous faces everywhere. John Inman, Wendy Richards and Jean Ferguson were all to my left and I couldn't take my eyes off John. He looked terribly ill and he had ballooned to an uncomfortable size. Today, I watch `Are you being served` most nights but we'll get to that. That night, Norman received a life time achievement award from the Water Rats. As we were leaving Norman went round with me to say goodbye, SB was nowhere to be seen, then I spotted her sat at a director's table, knocking back the red wine. I watched for a minute and she was flirting like no one's business, I remember thinking `she's up to something`. I got them back safely to Epsom and drove home, reflecting on what a beautiful evening we had. The next day I telephoned SNW to see if he was ok and he was feeling a little unwell. The next day he had to see the doctor. I was invited back down to see him and took a friend with me, SNW was thrilled to see me and I was chatting with him for a good hour. I noticed SB had got no patience with him, snapping at everything he said. I thought she must be having an off day.

After the success of my fashion show I had become great friends with Darran, he brought my show to life and he brought me back to life. I had been pretty obsessed with illness and hospitals. I had never regained my confidence after the verbal abuse from my ex and Darran came along just when I needed a friend. There has never been anything sexual with Darran, he is just a great mate. He made me laugh everyday and we went out often. He was always on the pull and as we both liked different types of men we were quite successful. It wasn't long until I asked Darran and his partner Daniel if they wanted to move into the spare room. After a few weeks of thinking they took me up on the offer. The day they moved in the house became a tip but we soon got everything in its place and `Dixi` my little dog loved the company and attention of course. At this time I started driving for JC, she was running a few gigs every year, mostly the NEC in Birmingham but also in the capital and going north to Manchester. These gigs are memorabilia venues, meeting famous people, buying autographs, stalls of rare items, comics, DVDs and dolls. One of the gigs for JC was driving Sarah Douglas to the NEC, she is famous for the `V` series and playing one of the baddies in Superman 2. I was surprised to learn she lived within miles of my house and I had passed her place on numerous occasions. I spent two days with SD, she is lovely and a down to earth woman. I am afraid I told her my life story before we had even reached the M40 but we became friends, I met her a few times after that weekend.

I had a phone call from SB that week, she wanted me to drive SNW to a small gig in Birmingham and then to take him to stay with some friends for a few days whilst she had a break. I duly picked them up from the airport. On the short journey to Birmingham I could see SB was preoccupied. I asked her if everything was ok and she said yes so I left it, changing the subject to Norman's gig. He was to meet some people who had raised some money for Manx Mencap. When we arrived at the venue I helped SNW from the car, he looked tired but there was something else I couldn't put my finger on. After the initial reception, he got up to sing a few songs and as I was watching him I realized he had ballooned, his face and belly were double the size.

I turned to SB and said "What are you feeding him? He's getting fat." Seeing her face I quickly added " Mind you he looks well on it."
She grinned and said "I've not always got time to cook a meal, sometimes it's easier to pass him the doughnuts."
I didn't say anything.
At around 9.30pm I drove them to Solihull and dropped them off, arranging to pick them up in three days. On the 3rd day and in the daylight, I couldn't find the house I'd previously dropped them off at, it looked different in the dark. I was cruising around for a good thirty minutes until I saw Norman waving his arms frantically at me in the mirror. He really did look like his film characters and I just couldn't stop larking about with him. I kept stopping the car and then pulling away as he got close, I really expected to hear "No No No Mr.

Grimsdale!" I got them back in time for tea, SB spent the majority of the time on the phone so I didn't have much of a conversation. I joined them for a cuppa, SB was asking me if Norman's agent had paid me for the journeys I had done. I never really spoke to her about money but at that time I was a bit skint and even if she could get me the fuel money I would be grateful. She said she would sort it out.

Rosie was still working for the Orphanage in Sierra Leon, she was always battling to help them, raising money wherever and whenever she could. Of course she still had the Rolls Royce and of course, I and Norman still loved it. She had been arranging a big gig at the Hilton in Warwick, a bit like `An evening with...`. Tickets were sold to a few hundred people to have a meal and to be entertained by SNW. Norman agreed to do it and Rosie got on with selling tickets and arranging everything. He was to fly in and do the gig, leave early that night to be back at his Epsom flat ready for the next day. I was to do all the driving. I am a little bit of a control freak, not obsessively but I like to be the organizer. I was happy that Rosie had organized this gig but I knew there would be some difficulties and I knew Rosie hadn't dealt with SNW or SB. I had been around for a while and I had got used to Norman's way and his routines. I had kind of got used to SB too, albeit she was unpredictable. I had been given permission to give Rosie Norman's telephone number, I thought if Rosie wants to go through the day's events with SB, at least the day will run smoothly. I heard from SB to say everything had been sorted and I spoke with Rosie and she said everything has been explained to SB, they were both happy.

About two weeks before the gig, things started to kick off, somehow communication had broken down. The first I knew was a phone call from SB asking me if we were using the Roller. I said we were and she asked me who was paying for the fuel, I told her Rosie was paying.

"Why? Is that ok?" I asked

"Oh yeah Steve, I was just thinking why are we rushing back? We may as well stay the night at the hotel and we can go to Epsom the next day."

I don't know why but I caught a smidgen of arrogance in her voice but I told her I'd relay the change of plans to Rosie.

"Ok Steve. Oh by the way, if you speak with her, tell her we will need a room each, she will have to book and pay for it herself."
I agreed to tell Rosie. I spoke with Rosie, she agreed to book them in.
A few days later I got another call, it was SB. " Steve, I know we are flying over next week but will you tell Rosie that SNW wants to come by helicopter. His mates on the island have offered to fly him direct from his house to the hotel. Also Steve, she will have to book and pay for another room for Norman's friends". I was a bit worried but I agreed to relay the message, understandably Rosie was furious. To pay for SNW and SB was expected but to pay for another room for his friends? I was asked to ring SB and explain to her that this was a charity gig and we want to raise as much money as possible. Dipping into it to pay for extra rooms is eating into the pot. I telephoned SB and once again relayed the message, this time SB was furious. "Remind her Steve, she's getting a fucking star for free and we want breakfast with the rooms. If she's not fucking happy, tough, we will call it off." I told Rosie about the threat, I could see she was feeling the strain but she had no choice and booked the extra guests in, including breakfast. I went through the day's events again incorporating the changes, it actually was less driving for me and I was quite grateful. I also reminded Rosie that at least she had no flights to pay for and would probably be in pocket. I asked her if the events had been cleared with SB and she told me yes. "I went through the whole thing with her", she assured me.

The day had arrived, poor Rosie was in a fluster making sure everything was going to plan. I was to pick SNW up from a nearby farm and bring him straight to the venue. To this day I will never forget the sight of that helicopter high in the sky circling around and coming down to land in the field. It was bright red and high, not at all what I expected. As it landed, SNW recognized me and started to lick the inside of his window, licking it like a delicious lolly pop. SB appeared first, she looked stunning I thought, very well dressed. Next appeared SNW, he came running over to me. "Allo Steve" he said, shaking my hand. I could see SB was talking to a smart looking couple, she brought them over. "Steve, these are Norman's friends L and E. E owns the helicopter, he uses it daily, L is his wife." I shook their hands and they all got into the Roller. I sent a text message to Rosie to say we were on our way.

As we arrived at the hotel there were press at the front doors, along with Rosie and her partner Colin. As soon as Norman got out of the car the cameras started flashing. Rosie approached SB and Norman and a few photos were taken. We went inside towards the huge reception room where there were about 100 people standing around. They all turned and started clapping, SNW did his usual trip. As the crowd parted I saw a sign which read `Photo with SNW £10`. I looked at SB but it was too late, her face had changed.

"What's that? Norman can`t pose for all those photos, he`s tired". I turned to Rosie but before I could say a word SB said, "I'm taking SNW to his room, he needs to rest for a hour".

Rosie said "You can`t do that, these people are waiting," but SB took hold of his arm and with friends in tow they went to their rooms. I sat down with Rosie.

"Did you tell her about the photos? You never mentioned it to me" I asked her.

"Yeah Steve, I told her there would be a few photos to raise money" she said.

"A few, SNW is in his 90`s. He will do it because he won't let people down but you'll only have an hour. I will have to talk to SB to see if she agrees", I replied.

I telephoned SB, she agreed that Norman would do about an hour of photos and then we would have to get on with the meal and speech because she wanted him in bed for 10.30pm. I think most people in that hotel had a photo with SNW, Rosie had organised the routine perfectly, I took the £10, they got in the chair and everyone smiled. Sometimes Norman pulled his face jokingly. The guests were led in to the reception room and shown to their tables, an hour later they had the photo in a sleeve. The last photo was of me, I took all the cash out of my bum bag and had a photo with Norman holding the cash. I have the photo on my stairs today, Norman's face is priceless. Rita had made loads of Wisdom cards to sell in reception. They joined me on the top table, R&R, me, SNW, Colin and Rosie, SB and their two friends. Everyone was sat down, about 200 people, they had all paid for the privilege to hear SNW sing, tell his life story and generally entertain. We were halfway through the meal when Norman turned to me and whispered, "Steve, I think I have forgotten the words, can I sing it to you? Tell me if I've got it wrong." With that he started singing `Up In The World`. Those five minutes will stay with me for the rest of my life, he practiced and struggled and within those minutes he got the song word perfect in my ear, I loved this guy.

The other part I remember is a guy pestering SNW for an autograph whilst Norman was eating his soup. I politely told him to come back later but he was adamant.

I whispered to Norman "This guy isn't going away, what do you want me to do?"
Slurping through his soup he slowly turned to me with a big grin and said, "Tell him to fuck off Steve"
He said it so loud everybody around us burst out laughing and the guy took the hint and went back to his seat. He was back within thirty minutes though and Norman signed for him. Norman kept his head down but he was looking at me, still grinning. Norman told a joke that night, given to him by Ray. It was about me driving and being a hairdresser.
"Why did you get Steve to drive you around Norman?" Ray asked
In front of everyone Norman said " I like Steve driving me around because he's a hairdresser so naturally he knows all the short cuts"
The audience burst out laughing, Norman was in his element and so he continued and told a few more joke stories and then sang a little more. After the meal he pulled the raffle, insisting on kissing the female winners, and at 10.30pm sharp SB took him by the arm and took him to his room. She had a face like thunder but I didn't care, he had a good night. The audience had a good night and Rosie, well poor Rosie she finally started to relax and as you can see by the film from that night she rather enjoyed the grape juice but good on her, she pulled it off. The above mentioned film was made by Rosie's friend, he put together the whole event. He made a cracking job of it and I know Norman's still got a copy today.

The next morning I met SNW and SB in the breakfast room, their friends in the helicopter had left early, apparently! SB had changed her mind and now she wanted to go to Epsom after all, I drove them home. All the way back, SB was slagging off the previous night, I didn't comment but I knew Rosie had done well. I did start to wonder if the whole change of plan fiasco had been planned and maybe SB just fancied a piss up with her friends. I was offered a coffee at the flat. I sat with Norman for an hour or so whilst SB made up the beds. I was asking SNW about the previous night, whether he had enjoyed it and what he thought of the food.

Norman looked at me confused, "I don't know Steve, was it good? I don't remember, did I make everyone laugh?"
"Yeah Norman they laughed, it was a good night" I said, I was beginning to worry.
I had been told he was losing his memory a bit but this was the first time I had really seen it. I held his hand and stroked it, he just stared at the TV with a blank look on his face. I said goodbye and drove home. All the way home I was wondering if I'd ever see him again, it seemed a very long drive.

Boy Of The Moment

Darran and Daniel were still living with me. My house had become a mess and it was depressing me so I had a word with the boys and they agreed to keep it cleaner. I remember coming home one day and the hoover was in the middle of the lounge, Daniel was watching TV. I asked him why it was there and he said "You asked me to hoover, I have but you never asked me to put it away". I blew my top, well blew it as much as I do, I hate confrontation. It's not that I want to avoid face to face contact, it's just I didn't want them to hate me or think I'm a bully. Truth be known I can be tough but only when I think fair is fair.
I had been talking to my parents about moving abroad, we wanted to live in the sun somewhere. My mates T&G were in Malaga and they settled in quite well. They chose to live in a proper Spanish village and I liked the idea of it, my parents agreed. We made a date for moving in two years but first we had to save some money, we all wanted to go over with at least 4k in our pockets. I had written to SNW twice and I had no reply, I followed up with a phone call but no reply. I was getting quite worried.

Often when I wanted to relax I would go with Darran to the gay sauna in Birmingham, it wasn't for sex although it obviously happened. I loved a good thirty minutes in the Jacuzzi, ten minutes in the dry sauna and then ten minutes in the steam room. I would always finish with a shower and a coffee. I always liked the saunas in Birmingham, when all is said and done at least you got to meet people, warts and all. I was in Unit 2 in Brum when I was being eyed up by this tall, dark slim guy. He was quite young and very sexy, we got chatting and I found out he was French. Well technically not French, but French (Confused? I was). He was from the Reunion Island, near to Mauritius. They are French speaking apparently and part of the EU. We chatted for a while and we decided to go for a drink, I had almost forgotten about Darran. I assumed he was in the sauna but as we got outside he was standing there smoking a fag.

Looking at `Renaud` he said, "Who's that?"

"Oh this is Renaud, I met him in the sauna" I said to him.

Laughing, he said "You're supposed to shag them and leave them behind, not bring them home."

We all had a chuckle as we went to the bar, we swapped numbers and I left. The day after I was flying to Spain, I needed a holiday. It was a last minute decision to fly out to see T&G, since mentioning the idea of moving out there they had got as excited as me and invited me to stay with them for a fortnight. I sent a message to Renaud promising him I would stay in touch.

Arriving in Spain was great, although I've always had a health obsession with planes. I was still scared of flying but this time I just relaxed all the way. The smell and heat hit me as the plane doors opened, it was a wonderful smell. Trevor picked me up from the airport and we drove to their house, where Gary had already got the kettle on. The village is Churrianna, a beautiful, old Spanish village. I soon discovered the village, in particular the best coffee shop in town, selling the best cakes. We went to the coffee shop every day, well I was on holiday and coffee and cakes are my weakness. Every afternoon we went out, normally to Torrimelinos or Arroyo del la Miel. I would buy all kinds of tourist shit, you name it I would buy it. When I discovered the 99c shop that was it, I was sorted. Early tea time I would go to the beach, it was a little cooler around 5pm, Trev would take me and pick me up around 7. The beach was always full of families but a mile up the sand was a nudest beach, this was my scene. I loved it, the sun beating down on the naked bodies around me. I am never embarrassed, the odd one out is always the guy that leaves his trunks on but walks through to see the talent. Trev would pick me up on the dot and we would go home to eat our only cooked meal that day. It was so hot you didn't really want to eat.

Night time was either the local bar or the Gay clubs in Torri. I had a few drunken nights in Torri, one in particular was a birthday party for one of T&G`s friends. I ended up getting very drunk, licking cake off a young lad's face, spewing up all over some flower beds and then sitting topless in the middle of this club. I was sitting on the steps in between some clubs, my head was crazy, my heart was fast and I was sweating profusely. I was there for nearly 2 hours, although I knew T&G could see me from where they were sitting (outside a Bear's bar), I didn't feel unsafe or threatened, in fact people were asking me in English and Spanish if I was ok and if I needed anything. I remember the young guy dropping something in my drink but without actually registering it, I drank it. Before I knew it I was in this different world and it wasn`t very nice. I sent a text message or rang Renaud every day whilst in Spain, that was the only day I didn't message him. I think we declared our love on the second week. Bearing in mind I had only met him a few days earlier, I definitely felt something for him and wanted to continue with this new relationship.

I spoke to Renaud just before I boarded the plane back to the UK. I told him to let me get home, have a quick shower and I'd drive over to see him the same night, I was landing at 11pm. I did as planned, I knew he was excited for seeing me and vice versa. I had bought him a bottle of bubbly and a nice watch. I had the shower, left some fags for D&D, had a quick kiss and cuddle with Dixi and by 12.30am I was passing the airport I'd just landed at, this time on my way to Birmingham. I messaged Renaud to say I was on my way, no answer. I rang his phone, no answer. I arrived at his house and rang him again, this time he answered. He was so excited at me travelling over to see him, he fell asleep, typical. I have to say, five years on and he is still the only person I've met that can sleep anywhere, immediately. If Renaud says he`s going to sleep I can guarantee you within a minute he will be snoring. I enjoyed my holiday but I'm always glad to be home. I got back to a letter from SB, it basically told me SNW no longer required my services and he thanks me, signed by SB. To say I was peeved is an understatement; the fact that she had signed it annoyed me.

R&R had been in touch, we were talking about meeting up for a day. R&R are wildly generous and for my birthday they had got me a ticket to join them in Brighton for the unveiling of the Max Miller Statue. They knew I knew Norman would be there, it would give me a chance to speak with him. I met R&R on the sea front, there was a crowd already gathered. We showed our tickets and entered the hall of the Royal Pavillion palace, it was stunning. The order of the day was a bit of singing and dancing by some older stars, the host was Roy Hudd, followed by a three course meal. In between dessert and coffee there was to be a speech and then an auction of signed items. As we took our seats, I suddenly jumped up. Rita took my arm, it was Norman and SB. I looked around and my heart sank, there he was laughing and joking, she had a big smile on her face. It didn't last long as I went straight over. Just as she caught sight of me, I put my hand out.

"Hi Norman, how are you? I've missed our laughter", I said
He turned to me and smiled, "Hi Steve, it's a long time since I have seen you, you've been ill haven't you?"
I didn't answer but rather changed the subject, I had the answer I was looking for. I told him I would see him later and took my seat again. I felt quite awkward that night, It was kind of strange being on the other side of the SNW party. I had a walk around in the interval. I met my old neighbor Dora Bryan, she was glad to see me. She had always kept in touch and whenever she released a book she sent me a signed copy. I also spent some time with June Whitfield, a few actors from Eastenders and a great man called George Mellie. George was very friendly, I had never met him before but we chatted like we had been mates for a long time. It was only later when R told me he was a bit of a flirt that I realized he was being friendly for other reasons, he was a bit tipsy. He did a spot of Jazz singing that night, I'm not a fan of Jazz but what he did I enjoyed. It was time for the speech and I'd already guessed it would be Norman. I can honestly

say I was as proud as punch when he came on stage and did his well rehearsed number. After he left the stage, I turned to R&R and said "Come on, I want to go and see him". They followed as we walked through the security, I explained I was his driver.

We went down to his dressing room and I knocked on the door, SB answered and she just raised an eyebrow when she saw me.

"I want to say hello to SNW" I said to her.

She barked back at me, "You can't, he's asleep, anyway you saw him upstairs."

Just as she said this I heard Norman, "Is that Steve? Hi Steve come in pal."

I walked straight past her and sat with my pal, it had only been a few months but he looked old. I congratulated him for what he'd done previously on stage. He said "Was I any good? I don't remember, what did I do?" He seemed a bit confused so I told him all about it. I could see SB staring at me out the corner of her eye while I assured SNW he was great on stage. After maybe ten minutes R&R came in to say hello and then SB butted in, a little more pleasant this time. "Come on, he's tired" she said, for once I agreed, he did look tired so we went back into the hall. That day I stood in the audience outside, I watched SNW climb onto the Max Miller statue and start to poke Max's nose, he then licked his finger and did it again. He was in his 90's and still climbing around, what a guy.

I was still dating Renaud, I had told him about my plans to tour Spain with my parents and he liked the idea of it. We started to save which is hard for me, I was born to shop. Sometimes I feel that whenever I have plans, I have health worries. One day I had got a niggling pain in my stomach, I thought it was something I'd eaten or maybe I was more than a little stressed and this didn't help. Overnight the pain got worse, I didn't want to disturb anyone because I knew I would be fussed over. Darran made a good nurse, bringing me coffee and fags but he also left me alone which is how I deal with things. This time it wasn't going away and the doctor was called. The doctor told me I needed to go to casualty; I wasn't keen to say the least. I didn't want Renaud thinking this was a regular occurrence and I didn't want SB to have an excuse to keep me away from SNW. Going to hospital was good for pain relief but my doctors all seemed 'operation happy'. They were always offering to open me back up but I wanted to find a way without the need of surgery. I shouldn't have worried, I was given some pain killers and slept a good 12 hours. The pain killer was in the thigh and I was out of it almost immediately. When I woke up I was desperate for a wee but there were no stomach pains and after successfully doing the obligatory toilet duties, the nurses told me I could leave. I was glad to get out of the place I have never been good with hospitals as you have already read.

After no replies from SNW or phone calls from SB I was getting concerned. I`d done enough driving and I felt lucky, even privileged but Norman was a friend and I decided enough was enough, so I emailed Johnny Mans. I told him about my concerns, being Norman's agent I thought he might want to know what was going on. Within 24 hours I had a phone call from JM, he was concerned also. He said SNW hadn`t seen any of his friends not even Patrick, a lifelong friend since the army. He asked if he could give my number to Kim, Norman's daughter in law. Within the hour Kim rang me, it felt strange to me. I had heard a lot about her and seen loads of photos of the Wisdom family but I'd never met them. I once met Jackie, Norman's daughter, but it was early when I'd first started driving and only for a few minutes.

Now reader, you'll have to bear with me now. I have to skirt around a few issues which cannot be mentioned or should only be mentioned if and when the time is right. Needless to say The Wisdoms were worried. JM was worried, I was worried, R&R were worried also but they took some convincing to really blow the whistle. I understand their worries, I had the same but my loyalty firmly stood with SNW. To cut a long story short, SB was sacked. I'm not going to tell you why, those of you who read the papers will probably remember but I was glad. She had tried to stop my friendship with SNW and she had a habit of 'losing' things I had sent.

Wit And Wisdom

I have to say Kim was lovely, we immediately got on and to this day she's a good friend, they all are. Within two weeks of all this kicking off Kim invited me to their house, she gave me the address and we arranged a day. The day is very memorable to me because Norman was there, the family were looking after SNW themselves until they could find a replacement for SB. I arrived at this beautiful farm house down a very scary lane near Brighton. I knocked on the door and this tall, average looking lady answered with a big smile. "Hi Steve, I'm Kim" she said, I knew instantly we would be friends. As she made me a coffee in the kitchen I looked around. I don't know what I expected, probably Wisdom memorabilia everywhere but there wasn't, instead it was normal, homely and relaxing. We were chatting about the last few weeks' events when I heard a noise behind me, it was Norman, he looked old and frail. I stood up to shake his hand, "Hi Norman, how are you? It's lovely to see you again."

He shook my hand as Kim walked over to him, "Norman it's Steve, he's been driving you around for a few years."
He apologised and said "Your face is familiar."
I felt like someone had shot me. We sat down and started chatting, within 20 minutes or so he was back on form, laughing and joking. He remembered what we had done and where we had been. After a second coffee Norman asked if we could go for a spin in the car, I looked at Kim.
"Yeah Steve, take him out for a few hours"
At this point, Norman jumped up, "Good ho" he said, "I'm just going for a slash", with that he scuttled off.
I thanked Kim for giving me this time, she said "I knew it was important to you Steve."
I thanked her again and walked into the hallway where Norman was, he was putting on the famous black jacket with gold buttons. We waved to Kim and we set off in beautiful sunshine to Brighton Marina.
I took Norman for a walk across the beach, people were waving, a couple asked for autographs and a few elderly ladies asked for a photo. Norman did his usual pose and stuck his tongue into his cheek, that naughty school boy look, he was great. We walked around the marina and had a coffee at Café Rouge. The whole time we sat there people were whispering `That's Norman Wisdom, that's Norman`, I could never understand why people were scared to say hello. Norman is the most normal approachable bloke you could ever

meet, I was amused to see the same people passing two or three times to catch another glimpse. I got Norman back after a few hours, we had a lovely day out and its one of my favourite memories.

Kim told me to ring her next week so I did, this time we arranged a full day out, I took Norman back to Brighton. This time I rang my old friend Dora Bryan. I told her I had SNW with me and asked if she wanted me to call in. She said it would be lovely to see him. I pulled up at `Claridges`, Dora`s House, it was previously a hotel and often used in the `Carry On` films. Dora`s son let us into the house, she had a beautiful full length window overlooking the sea. We sat there as Dora told us about filming with SNW, she was genuinely pleased to see him and Norman was obviously pleased to see Dora. I left them to chat for 30 minutes whilst I made conversation with her son. When we were leaving Dora made me promise we would call in again, I promised her we would. I took Norman down to the seafront again, back to Café Rouge and then we drove around Brighton in circles. "Just drive down here Steve, up there, yeah that one go down there", he said. We must have done every street in Brighton before I had to say to him that we needed to be getting back. As we were driving on the M23 I looked at Norman, he was sat back, shoes off and the sun shining through the windscreen. There was a huge smile on his face and then he saw me looking at him. "It`s beautiful Steve, just look, it`s beautiful." His arms were out, palms up showing me the scenery, I felt like the luckiest bloke alive. This legend was sat next to me, showing me his world.

Life in general was good, my kids were still living with Sue, their mother. She had married again to a man called Mick, he is a typical northern bloke and this is what my kids needed, a strong family unit. Although I had always been around and saw them often or as often as possible, my oldest had gone off the rails a little and my youngest was having difficulties at school, he had dyslexia. My relationship with Renaud was going well although we were looking forward to living together. Darran and Daniel were still lodging at the house but we wanted a home. The plans for Spain were on track, we were saving as much as possible. R&R helped me out a lot by buying some spare memorabilia I had accumulated, I reckon they contributed to nearly half of what I needed.

I was still driving for the other company; I did a gig to Birmingham NEC with Armin Shimmerman (Quark from Deep space nine, Star Trek). As I am a big Star Trek fan I was thrilled to be doing this job, Armin is a real gentleman. He thought I was quite a funny guy, he kept telling me I should be on stage. I told him driving a slapstick comedian around was making me as bonkers as the said comedian, he laughed. It's quite strange at these gigs; Armin had everyone from 5 yr olds to Grannies, all wanting an autograph and a photo. Armin made everyone welcome, even the fans dressed as `Klingons`. I spent a Friday, Saturday and Sunday with Armin. Apart from Norman, he is the most charming and caring person I have ever driven, the £180 tip helped of course. To this day we still email each other. When I drove Saran Douglas, a local artist presented her with a self portrait they had painted of her in character. The artist also did one for, both actors signed these pictures and gave them to me.

I drove another actress from Star Trek too, Robin Curtis. She was in the original and the Next Generation. She is absolutely beautiful and very elegant. Renaud came with me to the airport and then to the hotel, she was very friendly. We were both in awe of her and to be honest we were a bit full on, I was rather star struck! Robin also received a self portrait from the Birmingham artist, she signed the back and gave it to me, I didn't ask for it. I never told her about the other two but these portraits are rather special and they hold court in my house today on the stairway. I drove a guy from the `Monkeys`, I won`t tell you who but he wasn`t very chatty. The same day I drove a few Bond girls from the train station to the NEC. When it was time to take them back to the station I approached the guy from the Monkeys.

"I`m just going to take these ladies to the railway station Mr. so and so. I won`t forget you, I will be back in 30 minutes", I said.
He looked me up and down, "What's your name?" he asked.
I told him and he leant forward, "Steve, when I am ready to leave I'll fucking tell you, until then you`ll be waiting."
I never went back, I took the ladies to the railway station and I left. When I got home I rang my boss and told her. She said "That's fine Steve, if they talk to you like that, leave them". I drove the guy from the Hellraiser films for thirty minutes, his name is Doug Bradley. He

didn't need much make up to play his character but I have to say he is a nice guy, again the £20 tip helped.

I was beginning to gain a good relationship with my kids, they had met Renaud and they called him Mummy Renaud which still amuses me. Daniel and Jason were young men now, the difference I saw in them was phenomenal. Sue and Mick had dedicated their lives to ensuring my kids received a good education. Sue told me she fought with the school to get some extra help for Jason as his Dyslexia was holding him back. I often sit in my lounge when my kids are visiting and I find myself looking out the corner of my eye, staring at them. I can't believe they are the babies I helped bring into this world. I talk to my kids a lot about life and the fact that this is it, there's no second chance. This literally is your life and please for god sakes make something from it. I suspect a lot of fathers think like me, I can see a lot of difficulties for young people nowadays. There's a lot of pressure around and jobs are not easy to come by. When I was younger I wanted money, and we were taught if you wanted money you had to work for it. Yes, I've cleaned toilets for £5, you do it if you want the dosh.

I had a phone call from the Wisdom family, they asked if I'd like to spend some time with SNW. I jumped at the chance but best of all, they told me that in three months Ann is coming out of retirement to take back her old job with Norman, I was thrilled. I have a lot of time for Ann, she was always kind and courteous to me and she is great with SNW, she knew him inside out and Norman knew Ann. I picked Norman up from the Wisdom house, we had no idea where we were going. I just got onto the M23, London bound and then I had an idea. R&R had raised so much money for Manx Mencap in Norman's name, it would be nice to surprise them, so we did. We continued onto the M25 and drove to Kent, St Paul's Cray. We were about ten minutes away and I telephoned Rita to say I was passing and I'll be calling in. The surprise back fired because whilst I was speaking to Rita, Norman said "Is that Rita we are going to see? Oh good ho." She heard him and I had to confess and I told her I had a little friend with me. We first went to their shop, mainly as both of them were working and secondly, they had loads of photos of themselves with SNW holding huge cheques for Mencap, I wanted Norman to see them. He loved the shop, all the goodies, sweeties and photo frames. He walked out with a bag full of sweeties R&R gave him.

Every now and then Norman would tell me about the fantastic curries he had whilst he was in the army in India, he kept telling me how he liked a good curry. After R&R had closed the shop we went to a local Indian takeaway. It was great to see Norman enjoying his favourite food and he was great with the staff and customers, posing for photos. I had to get him back for 8pm and it was 7.30pm when we had finished the meal so we rushed off in the car towards the M25. Norman fell asleep so I took the opportunity to ring Kim to explain why we were going to be late. She was fine about it, told me not to worry which I was glad to hear. It was great that they trusted me with their father but I didn't want them to think I was unreliable or worrying. When I got to the house Kim thanked me, I said hi to everyone and left for home. All the way home I had the same stupid grin on my face I always had after driving him.

Within a week I had an email from Kim asking if I would be interested in driving herself and Norman to Cheltenham for a few days. He had a little gig booked and there was a meal booked with some friends of SNW. If my memory serves me right it was a gathering of guys and their partners who were in the 10th Royal Hussars with Norman, it was also the hotel where Norman's career kicked off. We were staying in a B&B, again friends of the Wisdom's. We were meeting Patrick there, a lifelong friend and thoroughly nice, funny guy. Patrick was also in the 10th Royals with Norman and later that weekend, Patrick told me he used to write for Ronnie Barker and others of that era. I picked Kim and SNW up and I had the journey planned in my mind; M25, M40 to oxford and cross country to Cheltenham, five hours later we arrived. I apologized for the long drive. Kim said to me "I thought it was a long way Steve, you should have taken the M5." Of course she was right, but I've always driven the way I've known, it just takes a bit longer sometimes. I never get lost, I just don't know where I am. Thank god for SatNav.

The first night we had to go to a small club near Evesham, I had been before with Norman so I knew the routine, it was a small village club and Norman had to do a bit of singing and socializing, it was very pleasant. Whilst Norman was in the club, Kim and I left him with

Patrick. We walked into the village to a nice bar and had a meal. It was nice to sit with Norman's daughter in law and talk about us, our lives and families. We duly picked everyone back up and got back to the B&B. Everyone socialized in the little bar and at about 12.30am we all retired to our rooms. For me, there was no retirement. I had arranged with Kim for us to go to my home town of Leamington Spa. The trouble is I wanted Renaud to be there and he was still living and working in Birmingham. I waited until everyone was in their rooms and I sneaked out the B&B and drove up the M6 to pick him up and take him to Leamington. Then I drove back to the B&B, I got to bed at 5am and I was up again at 8am.

That day I was knackered. On top of that Patrick's friend was coming with us, that meant 5 adults in my car which at the time was a C3. After an hour of driving we got to Leamington, we were going to a café where Darran was working. Darran was at work, Daniel and Renaud were meeting us there. We arrived pretty much on time, Daniel had been very excited to be meeting Norman, as it happens he was the first to meet him. As we entered the café Daniel stood up to shake Norman's hand. Norman looked at him said hi and then "Where's the toilet? I need a slash." Dan pointed the way and he was off. Renaud had no idea who Norman was, he had only seen photos from me and in his country they never showed the Wisdom films. He was excited though and he was so disappointed that the only photo we took which came out blurry was the one of himself and Norman. As we were walking back to the car, this guy caught sight of SNW and he came running over to grab our attention. "Please Norman, please would you say hi to my Nan on the phone? She loves you." Of course Norman did but then there was a crowd gathering and I just knew we would be there all day. I indicated to Norman that people were crowding around us and luckily he took the hint, ended the call and jumped in the car.

We got back to Cheltenham in time for Norman to have a sleep before we were back out again, all dressed up for his reunion meal. This was great, I wasn't driving (it was only round the corner) and I was invited. The meal was for about twenty people and conversation was easy. It was quite a posh restaurant and we had quite a few courses plus wine. By the end of the evening, we all seemed a little tipsy apart from Norman as he didn't drink but he looked tired. When the waitress came over she made the mistake of showing Norman the bill. Well, I have to say this goes down as one of the funniest meals I have ever had. Poor Norman had only had a soup and the bill was £122. He thought it was for him but it was for one of the other guests. "£122 for a fucking soup" he said at the top of his voice. He then repeated "£122!" We all burst out laughing, Kim calmed Norman down and the poor waitress didn't know what to do. We ended the night with laughter and walked home. Well, to be honest I staggered with the wine and sleep deprivation.

Before the meal we had some drinks in the reception and while we were drinking, this young man (maybe 21yrs) came over and introduced himself, he worked for the local newspaper. He asked Kim if he could do a little interview and she agreed. I was asked to sit with Norman through the interview, which I was thrilled to do and this guy asked Norman a few questions about his career and possible retirement. Norman answered everything and the guy thanked us, he asked if he could sit with us a little longer and Norman said yes.

Whilst in conversation he said to Norman "You are 90 plus now Norman, what would you say if some people said you shouldn't be driving at your age?"

I was just taking a sip of my whisky when Norman said "I'd tell them to fuck off!"

I sprayed my drink everywhere as I said, "That's off the record, right?"

The reporter said "Oh yeah" and he got up to say it was late and disappeared.

As we were all leaving I noticed this reporter outside on the phone, he wasn't cute so I didn't say good night. The next day it was in the Sun newspaper, 'Norman says fuck off to people commenting about his driving.' I couldn't believe it and of course, I had numerous phone calls from friends asking if I'd seen the newspaper and whether Norman really said that. Well yeah he did but i can tell you it isn't language SNW would normally use. As for me, it taught me a lesson. I now knew how reporters got their stories, I now knew not to trust them and how something random and innocently said can be sold to the tabloids and blown out of proportion. As it happens, I think most people found it amusing to read and within a few days it had all blown over.

Some More Words Of Wisdom

Ann was back, I immediately telephoned her to give her the full run down of the last few years whilst she had been away. She was pleased to hear from me and it was like we had never been apart. I had matured a little and I wasn't just a fan writing to Norman, I was now his friend and a family friend. I will always thank Ann, I think or hope she could see I wanted nothing from SNW. It's true, I over did the autographs for a while but then I was driving him around for free sometimes so we both gained something. I still have my autographs, I have over 800 but they're not all SNW. Ann invited me over to Ballalaugh, I couldn't really afford to go over but I loved the island and to see Norman in his house again was great. I decided to go and bugger the expense.

This time I went alone by boat, I wasn't going to fly on my own. I got to the ferry port at Liverpool in plenty of time. I took a tour of the city for an hour or so and I spotted an Ann Summers shop, I had seen them before but I'd never been inside. I decided no one knew me in the town so I went for a peek. I had been in some sex shops in the past and gay saunas but this was an eye opener for a high street store. I bought a little vibrator, I think it was called a 'Rabbit', two probes one for each.... anyway you get the idea. It wasn't for me, it was for a friend at college. Marge was a good friend, she wasn't married and always looking at blokes, always looking for that perfect match. We laughed all the time and I had promised her I would bring her something back from the island. I never said which island so I thought I'd give her this rabbit upon my return. Little did I know it would get me into trouble on more than a few occasions.

I got on board the ferry and settled down for the short journey, I bought a coffee and then put my bag on the seat to use as a pillow. I decided a kip would freshen me up and I sprawled out with my head on the bag. About a hour or so later, I woke and truly I had dribble hanging from my chin. I sat up abruptly to dry my mouth when on the floor in front of me was the Rabbit. Worst still, sat around me were a group of lads, all drinking. I didn't know whether to grab it or ignore it but before I could make my decision, this hooligan shouted "Hey mate, your vibrator's on the floor" and they all burst out laughing. I pulled out the Ann Summers bag and put the offending item back in. I wanted the guys to see the bag and for them to realize I had just bought it as a gift. This one guy kept staring at me, he was cute and quite muscly but he was scowling.

I took hold of my things and moved to the next bar, ordered a coffee and I settled down next to a window. After a few minutes this guy from the other bar approached me and sat down. "There you are" he said, "I have been looking for you". With a nervous smile I said hello. He started talking to me, he said he was from Liverpool and he was going to the Isle Of Man for a few days piss up with his mates and asked if I would like to join them. I declined and told him I was there on business. He asked me what business so I told him I was a Chauffeur, he seemed impressed. It was announced over the speakers that we would be arriving in 15 minutes. This guy suddenly pushed a little closer so that we were both facing the window. All of a sudden I felt his hand go across my thigh, onto my zip and before I could react he had my zip down. I pulled away and apologized telling him I wasn't like that.

He looked a bit pissed off but with a grin on his face he told me, "You would like it I know you would and I'd love to use that vibrator on you."

I made my excuses and stood up quickly, "I've got to go, my family will be waiting for me" and I left.

Now any other time I would have took him somewhere quiet but this time around I knew Renaud was at home and I was in a relationship. As I was walking off the Ferry I looked over to the lads, all pissed and all being rowdy. I couldn't see the cute one but as I turned back around he was there, standing right in front of me. He thrust some paper into my hand and kissed my cheek in front of everyone and walked back to his mates. On the paper he had written, `My name is Ian, I am staying at blah blah blah hotel, room 70, come see me tonight before 10pm`. I screwed the paper into my pocket and went to collect my hire car. I was only on the island for 4 hours as I had to be back on the boat at 8pm ready to leave for the UK. I drove to Ballalaugh, got my bag out of the boot and knocked on the door.

Ann answered with a big smile and asked me to come in. She told me she was baking a cake in the kitchen and to go through to the lounge where Norman was watching the boxing. I went through and saw the back of his head. As I walked around the chair I said "Hi Norman, its Steve. How are you?" To my horror he was sat with his head laid back, his hand on his heart and his eyes rolling upwards. His mouth was open and his tongue was hanging out.

I took hold of his hand "Norman, Norman are you ok?" His eyes blinked and then closed as one re opened and with a big jump, he was on his feet laughing his socks off.

"Steve, I got you. Did you think I was dead?"

With a sigh of relief I said, "You little bugger you had me there I thought you had popped your clogs."

We both burst out laughing. Ann came through into the lounge carrying a tray with tea and a fresh cake. She must have seen us both dribbling because she cut us both a great big slice. I`ve always appreciated the kindness Ann gave me, it was nice to have her back. SB never offered anything. On numerous occasions I had to make coffee for me and Norman, she just used to disappear, which wasn't a bad thing I guess.

I told Ann what Norman had done to me. She told me that on various occasions she would walk into his bedroom and he would pretend to be dead. If he went to the garage and she followed after him, he would lie on the garage floor with his fingers stuck in the electricity socket, pretending he had been electrocuted. I had a good few hours with Norman, he was keen to put a film on so we chose one of his films, my favourite, `On The Beat`. Although I'd done this before with Simon and Doris, even years on it still felt strange. Norman was telling me about filming in Leeds and how they had to get permission to close some streets and to wear police uniforms. He said the film was great to make as there was a lot of messing around on and off the set. I took the opportunity to ask him about his falling over. I had seen him on stage in earlier years and he always ran across a room and jumped on a piano, losing his balance and falling off it.

"Norman, did you ever get hurt whilst filming or whilst on stage throwing yourself around?" I asked.

"Oh yeah" he said "sometimes I would land funny or sprain my wrist or elbow but as I landed I used to think of the cash they had paid me. Somehow it never really hurt that much then."

Good answer I thought.

The time had come for me to leave, it had been a bit of a rushed day but I had thoroughly enjoyed it. Norman asked me if I wanted to stay the night but I had to decline, I had a ticket booked and the car had to be back. I had a couple of DVD sleeves with me and asked Norman if he would sign them. I took them out of the bag but as I tugged at them the dreaded Rabbit Vibrator flew out of the bag and on to the floor. I quickly went to grab it but Norman had got it first, I snatched it from his hands telling him it was a novelty pen. He asked if he could have it but luckily Ann came in at the right time and said "No you can't have Steve's pen Norman, ignore him Steve he always wants other people's things". I sighed a relief and thanked god she didn't ask to see the novelty pen. I left with a goodbye and a big piece of cake Ann had put into some foil for me.

As it happens the Ferry was delayed by an hour so I spent some time looking at the shops albeit limited on the Isle Of Man. Within no time the call came through to say we could board. I gathered my things and went to board, the security is minimal for visitors to and from the UK and I had never been stopped before but this time I was called over to Customs. They told me they were doing spot checks and asked me to take off my coat and open my bag. I did as they said whilst telling them about the great day I had had with Norman, he looked at the DVD sleeves in the bag so I assumed he believed me. Of course he had to go through my clothes and then he pulled out the vibrator. "What is this?" he said. I was just about to tell him it was a novelty pen when he sniffed it and then turned it on. I nearly died of embarrassment. I explained it was a friend and he put it back (with a smirk on his face) and let me through. I just knew he couldn't wait to tell his friends. The journey back was uneventful due to the fact I fell asleep again and woke up 30 minutes before reaching the UK. I got myself a coffee and stood outside to smoke a fag, it was quite a calm evening as I sat there overlooking the coast of Liverpool. As the boat got closer to the dock it started to rock around a little, I heard a noise under my seat and looked down. As I did, the Rabbit Vibrator rolled across the floor so I picked it up and put it back in my bag. We had gone through a lot in 12 hours, me and that vibrator. I got home around 1am and I was knackered so I decided to go straight to bed.

The next day I took my bag with me to have my photos of the previous day developed. I took the camera out of my bag and yes, you've guessed it, out popped the Rabbit. This time it rolled across the floor in the shop. I decided enough was enough and I ignored it but as I was fiddling with the machine to develop my photos when I got a tap on the shoulder from this little old lady.

"Is this yours?" she said holding the vibrator.
I told her "No, but I think it's one of those novelty pens, you keep it. They are quite good."
With that she shrugged her shoulders and put it in her pocket. I would love to know what she did with it. One thing's for sure, she would never have known it had been on a Ferry to the Isle Of Man and back, almost getting me a beating, rolling on Norman Wisdom's floor and getting me caught at Customs. I miss that Rabbit.

Dec 2005

Oct 2010

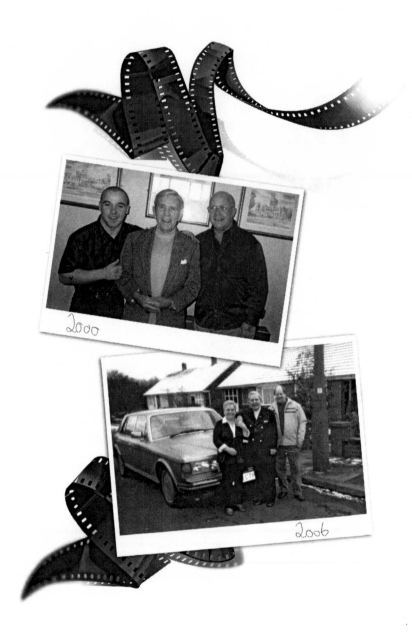

Things were getting serious with me and Renaud, he decided to move in with me and my lodgers. It was nice having a partner living with me and I detested the drive to Birmingham and back. A few days later Ann telephoned me, Norman was doing a gig on a ship, he was sailing from a port near Truro to the Norwegian Fjords and she asked if I would like to drive them. I said yes, got the details and booked the time off. Renaud was starting a new job in Leamington, I was glad he had finished working in Birmingham as the journey was a killer. What I didn`t realize was that I would be driving him to work most mornings because he couldn`t drive. We decided he should start taking driving lessons. Apart from the fact I would get a lay in, I wouldn't be the only one driving around Spain when the time came to take our grand tour. He started with a nearby driving school and I was taking him out at night time to give him extra confidence. Of course this didn`t work because I am quite impatient and spent most of the lessons arguing.

Renaud had been working a few days when my health took a nasty turn, I had no choice but to get myself to casualty and quickly. I rang Darran at work to tell him where I was going, he in turn told Renaud who worked opposite him. In casualty I was told that the pouch was collapsing in on itself. I was given some pain relief and a bed on a ward. As usual, the pain relief knocked me out and when I woke I was having a blood transfusion. In fact it was nearly over, as whilst I had been out of it they had given me 2 units of blood. Renaud was there, along with Darran and Daniel. I felt fine but it was a Thursday and the nurses told me I wouldn`t be out until after the weekend. Given my past experiences I knew I wouldn`t last five days, I actually lasted one night. Early morning I pulled out the needle and packed my things. As the nurses were busy with breakfast and bed baths, I walked out to my freedom and that's how it feels to me, freedom. Renaud went crazy at me but to be fair he didn`t know it was a habit of mine. I explained how I become trapped and panicky in hospital, I can cope for 24 hrs max but then I have to get out. I found out from Renaud that when he was working, Darran came over to say I was in hospital, Renaud had to think of an excuse and told his bosses that his `wife` was in hospital. They had seen me visiting Renaud and calling in for coffee so they had come to the conclusion that Renaud was married and I was his bit on the side. You can see how gossip starts can`t you? We still laugh at that one.

I picked Ann and SNW up from Epsom. Patrick was there also but no one had told me, so the car was rather cramped with four adults and luggage for free, as usual Norman sat in the front. We planned to be there for 1pm and the time was 9am. After three hours of solid driving I was getting agitated, my SatNav was taking me in circles and I had an hour to get him to Falmouth. When I checked my SatNav, I realized something was wrong, Ann had given me the wrong postcode. We entered the right one and I was horrified to find we were over 60 miles away. I drove frantically, worrying that the boat would leave without him and we arrived just after 2pm. As I drove onto the dock, a huge cruise ship was stationary with a white marquee on the dockside, staff were all in uniform and serving champagne to guests as they arrived. I indicated I was carrying Wisdom and they instructed me to pull up right outside the marquee. As I jumped out to open the doors and get the luggage, a nice lady in uniform came over. "You timed that just right" she said, "the guests are on board but we're delayed until 4pm." I could have screamed at her, I had been driving like a lunatic for over an hour, they could have telephoned Ann`s mobile to say there was a delay. SNW and Ann thanked me and Patrick shook my hand. "See you in three weeks Steve" he said and within a minute they had gone through to board the ship.

I was tired but I had to get home so I decided to break the journey up a bit, by driving for about an hour towards the motorway and taking a kip in the car before resuming the rest of the way. I drove as planned and by 4pm I was starting to see signs for the M5. I pulled into a garage and bought a sandwich and a coffee then drove down the road until I found a place to stop. It was late November and getting dark. I ate my sandwich, drunk half my coffee (the first for 8 hours) and settled back in my seat to rest my eyes. I woke around 8pm and started the car because I was freezing. I turned on the lights because it was pitch black, to my horror I could only see white. In the few hours I'd been asleep, the weather had changed to a good two feet of snow, I couldn't believe it. I still had a good 4 hour journey ahead of me and that was in good weather. I was driving home to Leamington not Epsom. I hit a road block, the traffic was backed up and from what I could see the motorway was closed, although I hadn't got that far. I sat in that car for 7 hours and moved around 3 miles, everyone around me was stuck and all in the same situation. All I had to drink was my cold coffee and some mints to eat. I got home early hours, I was exhausted. The journey had cost me double in fuel, it was further than I had imagined and I had to do it again in 3 weeks. I normally look forward to driving Norman but this one I was dreading. I telephoned Kim to tell her I needed some fuel money, she said she would sort it out for me.

I have a good friend called Dave, he is in the army. His car was bigger than my own (size isn't everything) and he agreed to swap cars with me as the time had come for me to pick Whizzy back up. Dave is a bit of a hero to me but you'll read why later on in the book. I set off back to Falmouth, this time I was taking no chances. It was the day before they were due and I had booked into a local hotel. I also took sandwiches and a flask with me but it wasn't necessary as the weather was nice for December. I set off in Dave's car, this time under my own instructions I arrived in Truro within 3 hours. I booked into the hotel and had a late meal. I couldn't sleep and it wasn't late so I decided on a practice run to Falmouth docks and back. If you have driven around this way you will know there is a series of steep hills towards the docks. I had driven my dummy run without any problems but when I was coming back down one of these hills, this car pulled in front of me. I braked, the whole back end started to skid sideways and I ended up across the middle of this dark lane. I pulled over very carefully to take a breath. Not realizing the temperature, I hadn't noticed that the whole road was covered in black ice, lucky escape I thought.

The next morning I drove 'carefully' to the dockside, the boat was already there. I made enquiries regarding SNW and he duly appeared with Ann and Patrick. This time everything fitted in the boot no problem and my guests had more leg room. We set off back for Epsom. Halfway, we stopped for a coffee and cake, I paid. Norman was doing his usual messing around, playing with the sugar but again, I was shocked at how old he looked. Ann could see I was worried "Don't worry Steve, the holiday has done him a world of good". I got them back to Epsom early afternoon. Ann made sandwiches and coffee whilst Patrick told me about the trip. Apparently SNW had been booked to do a little gig two or three nights a week, they also raised money on board with SNW signing autographs. The money they raised was donated to Manx Mencap. I set off home, arriving around 6pm. Again I was knackered, Renaud told me there was some post for me, I opened it and there was a cheque from the Wisdom's for fuel money, £30. I reckon it had cost me £70 in fuel three weeks earlier and £60 this time around. It didn't bother me that I was out of pocket, I enjoyed driving Norman and we enjoyed each other's company. It did bother me that they were out of touch with the cost or time or distance it took from Leamington to Epsom to Falmouth and then back to Leamington, to then do it again in reverse 3 weeks later.

It was around this time I became a qualified hairdresser, I had new friends, a different social life and I had Renaud. One of my new friends was a Spanish lady called Edith. She had a Barbers in my town and I often called in to see her, sometimes helping her out. She was quite famous for working in a Barbers called Paddy's, a local legend. Paddy once cut my hair, I was sat in the barbers waiting my turn. There were three barbers working away and an old chap on a stool drinking whisky, he was taking the money from clients. When it came to my turn he indicated for one of the women to take a break. He told me to sit in her seat and he came over to do my hair, still carrying the whisky. His hands were shaking badly, he looked like he had drunk a few whiskies that day and when he spoke to me, I knew he had. I was more than a little nervous but I can tell you he did a cracking hair cut. In fact I have rarely had such a good haircut before or since.

When he died, the barbers was closed down and Edith moved to open her own shop, taking most of Paddy's clients with her. She knew about my association with Norman and she was always asking me to bring him to the shop but it wasn't really his scene. I once did a hair cut at Edith's for a tramp that had come in. Edith took me into the back of her salon and said "Steve, will you do that one for me? Please, please", so I agreed to do it. I sat this man in the chair and gowned him. I asked him what he wanted and he asked me (through his gin soaked breath) to take off his beard and trim his hair. I took the machine to his beard, which made Santa's beard look like stubble. As I was shaving, I noticed something leather like near his skin. Worried I was going to cut him, I took it steady and edged my way in. The leather turned out to be a fried egg. Honestly, as true as I'm typing this he had nearly a full fried egg stuck to his face and the beard had grown through it, securing it to his face. With my reckoning, it had been there 3 months. Holding back the spew I continued, intrigued really and when I'd finished he looked half decent. No tip, all though he said "Thanks mate". I nearly asked him if he wanted to save the egg but I binned it. Edith was doubled over in the back, I was a caught between giggling and being sick. The smell did me in but I cleaned up like a professional and put everything in sterile solution. I've only ever cut one person whilst hairdressing. Whilst training I was cutting the hair of Alison, a bus driver friend of mine. She is always game for a laugh and whilst practicing one day, I cut her below the ear. She never said a word whilst I was trying to discreetly mop up the blood. When I had finished, I confessed about the cut. She said she never felt a thing and was surprised to look in the mirror and see this cut.

Alison came with me the next time I drove Norman. I had been asked if I wanted to drive him to the Grosvenor hotel in London. There's no story in driving him there but coming back, Alison came with me for the ride. Now anyone who knows Norman knows he's a ladies man and when he saw Alison and her bust, his eyes lit up.

When I introduced him to Ali (as I call her), he gave her a hug and a kiss and then nestled his face in her chest. Ali being Ali was thrilled at meeting Norman but she didn't know what to do when he warmed his cheeks in her bust. I can tell you she was doing the now famous `laughing like a school girl', pushing him away and pulling him back`. She's going to kill me when she reads this. We took Norman and Ann back to Epsom and Ann very kindly invited us in for a coffee. Whilst there, Norman signed a few autographs for Ali and her mum and I took a few photos for her. I've never met anyone like Alison, she has to be the hardest working woman I have ever met. She really will drive to the max everyday, 7 days a week if she can. I always have time for Alison she's a good woman and tolerates me all the while. I used to introduce Ali to friends or clients like this. "Hi this is Alison, a friend of mine. Don`t worry she used to be a man but the operation's going well", or "Hide your wallets guys, Alison's here." It was only a bit of `carry on` humour but she loved it.

I had a letter from Norman, he had been invited to a fund raising gig at the Grosvenor hotel in London. Included for me was a three course meal, I telephoned him to say I'd do it. The last few driving jobs I had done had covered the fuel but it was getting expensive so I had a word with Ann. She told me to bill JM for every job I did so I started making a record. Included were a few jobs I did with SB a few years earlier, at which time SB had told me to bill JM, JM being Norman's agent. Feeling better about the whole situation I made arrangements to pick up SNW, this time he was with a friend. I took them to the hotel and we arrived in good time for the meal. The Grosvenor is a beautiful place albeit expensive for me. Again we had free wine but I couldn`t drink as I was driving. The night had old style entertainment, Norman went on stage and did a few songs.

Coming back to the table he said "How did I do Steve? Did I get away with it?"

"Yeah Norman, you were great" I assured him.

In the room were quite a few stars, my kind of stars. Jean Fergusson is the most beautiful woman, she was there with John Inman who looked old and ill, Valerie Leon from the carry on films looked amazing and she was lovely when I was chatting with her. There were quite a few people from Eastenders including Wendy Richards who I was speaking with for quite a while. At the end of the evening, Norman asked me to take him round to all the tables to say goodnight and then we left with his friend to go back to Epsom. I thoroughly enjoyed this gig, I saw Norman in all his glory. He wasn`t impressed with the famous people around him, he was probably the most famous person there. I did notice they were all pleased to see him and they were genuine.

After quite a long period of driving, I decided I needed a break. Renaud had some family in the South of France so we made plans to visit. We invited my mum and Pete to come along as well and I decided I would drive us there; it would be good experience to drive abroad. In October 2005 we set off for Avignon. I had booked a hotel in Lyon so the plan was to drive to Dover, rest on the ferry and arrive in Calais early afternoon. Then we would drive all the way down to Lyon, rest until the next day and continue to Avignon. Everything went to plan, the toll roads were more expensive than we thought but we were on holiday so it didn`t matter. I was doing all the driving so by 8pm I was getting tired. The smog in the car was quite thick, my mum chain smoked all the way. It`s not her fault, some years ago she was in a bad accident so every time I went more than 50 mph she lit another fag and i`m a fast driver. I was smoking also, that and my Alison Moyet CD got me through the journey. We arrived in Lyon quite late and found the hotel. It was down a dark street on a housing estate, outside were burnt out cars and kids drinking cans of beer. We went inside to book in but the receptionist told us there was no electricity so we decided to find another hotel. We booked into a nice hotel in the town centre and I think I can safely say we slept all night.

After a hearty breakfast we set off around 8.30am and it was a big mistake. Now I have driven around France and Spain, as well as the full length of the UK but Lyon scared me. I had heard about the French drivers but I wasn`t expecting the chaos we were driving through that morning. People were swerving from lane to lane with no indication and all at high speed. Luckily we got through it quickly and 3 hours later we arrived at our destination. Renaud's brother and sister in law were living in a beautiful French village called L`isle Sur La Sorgue. They had booked us into a hotel which we thought was fabulous. It had an outside swimming pool with chalets around the pool, we were virtually the only guests and every day we would have breakfast and then jump into the pool. The weather was really nice for us 'English' but I think the hotel staff thought we were a little mad. We had a beautiful holiday, Renaud's family were really nice and we had a meal with them every day. Alex, Renaud's brother, didn't speak English but Marlene spoke a small amount. They have a sweet little girl called Mathilde and most days we took her for a walk, more of an excuse for me to grab a coffee at the local cafés. After no time at all, our holiday had ended so we set off for the long journey back. This time I planned to drive the full length in one day and to catch the late night ferry to the UK.

As I had done the route a week earlier, I had a little more confidence and we bypassed Lyon all together. We were about 50 miles from Calais when this French Policeman on a motorcycle started waving at us, indicating for us to follow him. We did as he requested. He took us from the motorway and along a lane where he stopped and came to my window. I`m not even going to attempt the language but Renaud understood everything. Apparently the device I had in the windscreen to detect speed cameras was illegal in France but we tried to explain that when we left the UK, it didn't work. I left it on as it told me the Kilometers we were traveling rather than guessing with my UK speedometer. He wasn't having any of it and told us to follow him to the services. When we arrived he told us to wait there. He came back after a few minutes and asked for the insurance papers, driving license and registration document. All this of course was in French which was double dutch to us; thank god Renaud was with us. I didn't give him my driving license because I had a feeling about this situation. I'm now glad I didn`t, because he refused to give me the insurance and registration documents back. He wanted 600 euros or he was going to confiscate the car.

Renaud was a real trooper and told him he couldn`t seize the car because there were two disabled people in it. He then popped his head through the window and told mum and Pete to act like they were disabled. I don`t know what the police thought but my mum had already got three fags on the go. Renaud decided to ring his brother who luckily was in the police, and after that conversation we were told we could go. The Policeman told us he was confiscating the device and a fine would be sent to my address. After we left, Renaud telephoned his brother again and he told us that the police cannot demand cash on the spot and he should not have confiscated the speeding device. We didn't care, we were free to go and we flew down the motorway for the last 50 miles. I think it's safe to say we were glad to be on board the ferry. It was an experience which we laugh about now but we were so grateful Renaud could speak French because he got us out of a potentially scary situation. We never did get the fine, funny that!

After that experience we were glad to be home. As usual, there was a pile of mail for me, one from SNW. He was asking me if I wanted to drive him, yet again, to the Grosvenor Hotel, it was a kind of Bafta awards and he was receiving an award. This time he told me I could bring Renaud. I picked him and Ann up from Epsom, both me and Renaud were in our full black tie and togs. I think David Dickinson would say "We looked right bobby dazzlers" and we did. Norman had his usual dinner jacket on and Ann looked her amazing self. This time Renaud and I were on a different table because Ann and Norman were on the top table. It was a lovely event, I remember being at the bar with Renaud and ordering an orange juice and a vodka and cranberry, the bill was £17 for the two drinks. I told Renaud to make good use of the free wine, these people could obviously afford it but to me it was outrageous. There was a series of awards, to the Eastenders cast, to the cast of Last of the Summer Wine and Norman got an award for his contribution to comedy. I was very proud to be driving him and he looked thrilled to bits.

GOING GENTLY

Things were changing in the Wisdom household, Norman's health was ok but his memory was getting worse. I remember thinking it was a bit of Alzheimer's as my Granddad had the same symptoms before he passed away. I was shopping in Leamington one day with Darran, Daniel and Renaud, the sun was shining and we had all had a good shopping day. We stopped for a coffee when my mobile phone rang, it was Kim.

"Steve, I don`t want to worry you but I don`t want you to read it in the press. Norman's ill, he`s in hospital. They have flown him to Liverpool from the Isle Of Man, we don`t know what`s wrong but I'll keep you informed."

I nearly burst out in tears, I could feel them welling up inside. I thanked her for ringing me, it was very kind of her to think of me. We went home in a daze, he is an important person in my life. I had grown to love him, like you would a grandfather. I telephoned Ann at Ballalaugh, she was crying on the phone. She was really worried and of course she was with him when it all kicked off, apparently he had pains in his chest and he was weak and lethargic. When the doctor arrived he made arrangements for Norman to be taken to hospital on the mainland. That night I didn`t sleep, I was thinking about the funny things we had gone through in 14 years, the situations we had got into and out of. The next morning Kim rang me, Norman had gone into surgery for a pace maker to be fitted. It was a heart problem but he would be ok, fingers crossed. Sure enough within days he was home on the Isle Of Man. I can`t be sure but if my memory serves me right he had a nurse move in for a while to help Ann out a little. I wrote him a letter and the reply I got said 'I am feeling well Steve, Ann has been great looking after me, she`s my tart. The pace maker is fine, I can hear it ticking but I'm going to have to go to WH Smith's for some batteries for it soon.' I was glad my old mate was back.

A few weeks later Ann had a break and Norman went to stay with Nick and Kim for a while. I asked Kim if he was well enough to go out for a drive and she said yes so we arranged a date. It`s funny how people are forgotten so easily. I can remember this lovely couple who had been writing to Norman and myself for a while but for the life of me I can`t remember their names. They lived near Gatwick airport I think but somehow we had arranged to have a meal with them at the Hilton near to where they lived. It was Renaud's birthday on the 28th of May, he was 22. It was the same day I was to take Norman out and we all met at the Blue Bell railway nearby. I picked Norman up from Kim`s house and met them there.

He looked great, very healthy and he was putting weight back on (Ann`s cakes I assumed). I chose the Blue Bell railway because I thought it would be an easy relaxing day for SNW but on the train he seemed agitated, sometimes getting quite awkward. Luckily it was only a 30 minute ride on the train and on the way back I asked him what he wanted to do. He told me he wanted to ride out in the car. Renaud and the couple went back to the Hilton, whilst I took Norman out for a little drive around, he fell asleep in the front seat so I took him back to Kim. I told her he had been quite awkward and she told me he is like this most days now. I sat with him in the lounge, he was still quite sleepy. I positioned myself on my knees next to his armchair and I stroked the old skin on the back of his old hand as he drifted off into a world of his own. I thanked Kim. She is always so kind to me and patient with him but I could see in her eyes she didn`t know what the future held for him. I said goodbye and drove to meet Renaud. In my head I thought this could be the last time I'll ever see him, little did I know.

A few weeks later I spoke to Norman on the phone, he was still at his family's house. He sounded good, back to normal and best of all, he wanted me to take him for a drive. I could hear Kim in the background advising him, I think she wanted him to think for himself and to organize a day out with me. He did organize a day, it was a drive to Brighton. I drove down to the house on the 6th of June 2006, it was a beautiful sunny day and I set off early to have a good day out with my mate. There had been a magazine called `Collect it` interested in my story, they wanted to feature my story and take photos of my collection. I asked Kim if she minded if they met with us down in Brighton. She agreed as long as Norman wasn`t expect to perform, I promised her it was just a chat. I rang the magazine and told them to meet us in Brighton at 1pm, Ann was the interviewer and Rob was the photographer.

Norman was in a great mood and we got down to Brighton for 11am so we decided to walk on the seafront. I took Norman to a local café where we were chatting about his films and he told me a few stories about his childhood, which I had heard before but I didn`t mind. He told me there used to be a woman in Brighton who was an actress in his films. I said "Yes Norman, it's Dora Bryan. We went to see her a few years ago, do you remember?"
He didn`t but he asked if we could go and see her again.

I telephoned Dora immediately "Hi Dora, its Steve. I`m with Norman and he`s expressed a wish to see you. Are you up for a coffee?"
She said "Yes Steve, when can you come to Brighton?"
I replied "We are here now, look outside your window in ten minutes and you will see us"
She seemed excited. We pulled up outside the house and Dora was waiting on the steps. She was having some work done and there was dust everywhere. For the first time ever I saw Dora grab hold of Norman and she planted a big kiss on his cheek, she then gave him a big hug. It was lovely to see them together, she obviously had a great deal of love and respect for Norman and he was thrilled to see her. On this visit I met Dora`s husband, he was sat in the window in a world of his own. He had a disorder, which I think was similar to Alzheimer's. We sat in the seafront conservatory for a good hour, Dora was telling Norman about her work and he was trying to remember. He had even forgotten Last of the Summer Wine which was a shame because Dora was in the current series. I took a few photos of the two stars re united.

It didn`t seem long before we had to say goodbye, I promised Dora we would call in again sometime and we left to meet the magazine people. We met Ann and Rob opposite the hotel, they were pleased to see us and took the opportunity to take a few photos of me and Norman on the seafront. It was a very windy day and I think Rob struggled to get a decent shot without Norman`s hair covering half of his face. We settled into the lounge of the hotel and Ann did her interview, whilst Rob took a few more photos. After a couple of hours and masses of tea and coffee we had to leave. Everyone was happy with the interview so we said our goodbyes and left Brighton to take Norman back to Kim`s. The trouble is, Norman wanted to see his old theatre again, which meant 30 minutes of driving around Brighton before I convinced him we needed to leave. I got him back to the house, made my apologies for being late `again` and told Kim about Dora and the magazine interview. I assured her everything went well and I left for home.

Two days later Kim rang me. Norman had been invited to the, yes you`ve guessed it, the Grosvenor Hotel for a meal, he was to receive his 4th life time achievement award. The date was the 10th of June

2006, The Heritage Foundation 11th Annual Dinner Awards. Both Nick and Kim were going and she asked if I'd like to drive them, they also invited Renaud. Of course I agreed. We had to dress up again, dinner jackets were sent to the dry cleaners and shoes were polished, this was to be a prestige event and we were excited. As it happens the plans changed a little. As this was to be a big day for Norman, the Wisdom's including Norman all went from nr Brighton in a Limo, myself and Renaud met them at the venue. This was one of those occasions where I was happy not to be driving Norman, it was a big day and I was glad the family were joining him. Kim, Nick, Jackie and his grandchildren were there, along with over 40 famous names. I watched as Norman was introduced and everyone stood up and applauded as JM walked Norman through the crowds and straight past me. I wasn`t really disappointed but I thought JM would have pointed me out to Norman. The meal was great, the entertainment was great, and everyone was drunk except me. A few of the girls from Eastenders fell in love with Renaud and he was thrilled to bits because Andrew Lance (Queer as Folk) was only a few tables way. Norman got up on stage and did a few songs, concluding with `I`m Forever Blowing Bubbles`. Some of the cast of Eastenders joined him. I was very proud.

I sent Renaud to get a few autographs, I nicked the menu from the table and he set off on his mission. He got over 35 signatures starting with Norman, Valeria Leon, John Inman, Wendy Richards MBE, Johnny Briggs, Jean Ferguson, Roy Clarke, Burt Kwok, Liz Fraser, Isla St Clair, and he even managed to follow Andrew Lance to the toilets to get his signature. I have to say some signatures on the menu I can`t work out but it's a great memory for us. I spent a few minutes talking to John Inman, his weight had doubled due to his illness and he struggled to even make conversation. I wish I had got. to know him better, bless him. Valerie Leon and Jean Ferguson are both favorites of mine and they always seem to have time for me, they have to be the most elegant women I have ever met.

That night JM was talking to me about a memorabilia event at the Radisson Hotel near Heathrow airport. I took the opportunity to remind him that I hadn`t been paid the fuel for the last 11 events I had done. I didn`t include mine and Norman's days out because they were personal and special days and I wanted to pay for them myself. He told me to send a bill to his office, I did. The Radisson was to be Norman's first signing event so we expected crowds. To top the bill, I was also driving an old friend of Norman's that day and to the same gig, Honor Blackman. She was famous for the Avengers and 007 but she also starred in a Wisdom film, The Square Peg. I can't even remember how I got that gig but I was thrilled to be driving her, I still have her mobile number. It's strange the amount of mobile numbers I have which belong to famous people but I would never ring them. If I needed to I would use them but there's a certain amount of trust with any person who gives you their number. I think with these famous people, they obviously trusted me therefore I would never abuse that trust.

I was given Honor's address but first I had to pick Norman and Ann up from Epsom, that was easy and routine now. We arrived nice and early to meet JM at the hotel, he was with his son who I instantly fell in love with. I took Norman up to this grand room. The fascination on his face was amazing, when he opened a cupboard door to see a TV behind it which had 'Welcome Sir Norman Wisdom OBE' displayed on the screen.

"I have a TV like that, in a cabinet at home" he said.

"I know Norman, I've seen it loads of times" I told him.

"Have you been to my house then?" he questioned me with a puzzled look

"Yes Norman, loads of times. Don't you remember?"

He just grinned. "Lucky sod aren't I?" he replied with a laugh.

I told him I would be back tomorrow as I had to go home and pick Honor up in the morning. He asked me why I wasn't staying at the hotel, I told him I couldn't. Truth be known I was fed up of waiting for the money owed to me from JM, over 2k now, it had built up. I couldn't afford to pay for a hotel for two nights, it was cheaper for me to go home and come back.

The day after I was outside Honor's house for 9am as planned. Ray was there in his car also, he was following me and joining me for the day. I rang Honor to say I had arrived and waited and waited and after 15 minutes she came down. I was driving my new Mercedes at the time albeit 'A' class but it was brand new and glossy black.

You're probably thinking how can he afford that and he's moaning about the 2k above, well it was the principle of the thing. If I had stayed at the hotel I would have probably had a few beers and told the truth a little too much. I opened the door for Honor, she looked amazing. She was dressed in black with her hair perfect and her jewelry sparkling, she looked a million dollars. It was only a 30 minute drive from central London to the hotel, when we arrived I could see masses of people all queuing up.

When we got inside we realized it was for Norman. I was chatting to Honor for a few minutes about Norman, she told me it was her idea to give Norman his nickname `Whizzy`, whilst they were filming The Square Peg. I dumped Honor to join Norman at his table, he looked tired but he happily signed autographs for everyone in the queue. About half way through the day I took Honor through to see Norman. She had expressed a wish to see him, obviously she was looking forward to it but he didn't remember her. I got a good photo of him kissing her but he did that with all the women. I took Honor back home that night, she was a little tidily on the free wine and somehow she had smuggled a bottle into the car. She was drinking it all the way home, we had a good laugh in that car, she's such a lovely woman. The next morning I picked up Ann and Norman and took them back to Epsom. Ann was telling me Norman had gone for a wander in his sleep at the hotel and at one point all the staff were frantically looking for him. They found him walking down a corridor the other side of the hotel, I had visions of him doing the Charlie Chaplin walk. I have one regret from that weekend, there was to be another star there that day. Well a star to me, her name was Millvina Dean. Millvina was the last survivor of the Titanic, the faithful ship which sank in 1912. I was looking forward to meeting her, she had wrote to me a few years earlier expressing a wish to meet SNW, I was trying to arrange a date when this gig came along which was perfect. Unfortunately she had to cancel the weekend due to ill health. I did get an autograph from her a few weeks before she died in 2009, I keep it in pride of place in my house. I regret not making more of an effort to meet her.

My children were now a big part of my life, visiting often. If I was in Yorkshire I would visit them or meet them at my Dad's bungalow or my Mum and Pete's house. My Dad got on well with my eldest son because they have a love of guitars. My Dad would often play the guitar for us and on one occasion he gave Daniel one of his collection. Jason was now working as a landscape gardener and he was volunteering for the Elsecar Heritage Trust, restoring old steam trains. I had been offered another day out with Norman. Kim asked me if I wanted to bring him up to my town to meet some of my friends. After all, they had all heard about our tales from me but a lot of them hadn't met him. This coincided with Edith wanting someone to officially open her Barber's shop, albeit it had been open over 3 months.

I picked Norman up quite early, Rosie had given me the gold Rolls Royce (she's so kind to me) and of course, Norman and I loved it. We drove up the motorway without much traffic so I was able to get some speed. Norman asked me to do 100mph so I did briefly (sorry Rosie) but then took it back down to 80. We got into Leamington and to my house for 11am. My kids were visiting so it was nice for them to spend some time with him, Renaud was working in town. Daniel's parents were also visiting so they got to see him, along with my neighbors, as Norman actually knocked on their door to introduce himself. I have great neighbors, Sheila is to my left and Brian and Josie to my right. In the corner is Alan and Abi, Alan has a beautiful motorbike and as we arrived Norman spotted it, of course he had to have a look. When we eventually got in the house, my kids had put a SNW film on the TV so Norman and my kids sat on the couch to watch the film, it was called 'Trouble In Store'. I made a coffee and sat opposite them, I was thrilled to be watching the film with my kids and Norman sat between them, although as usual he fell asleep. I had forgotten my date with Edith's salon, she rang me to see where we were. I told her we would be another 30 minutes. Edith had advertised Norman's visit so I was dreading the crowd. I had however told Kim this and we agreed that people would have to give a small donation for an autograph, the money going to Manx Mencap. I woke Norman after 30 minutes although he opened his eyes and told me he was playing, he wasn't really asleep.

After drinking his cold coffee, we set off on the 2 minute drive to Edith's, we were still in the Rolls Royce. Daniel and his parents went ahead, I took my kids and Norman. As we were driving down Clemens Street, I could see about 50 people outside the salon. Norman said "Are they waiting for me?" I told him yes and he smiled and sat up in his seat. The crowds parted as we pulled up, I told Norman to wait a second. I directed my kids to stand either side of him and walked round to open his door, as I did he jumped out. With his arms opened wide above his head, he started singing `Don`t laugh at me`, everyone started clapping and cheering. We went inside the salon and Edith posed for photos with SNW, pretending to trim his hair. My kids were like security guards, letting people through one by one. We limited autographs to one each and had a box on his table for donations. We took £70, which isn't bad for ten minutes work. After doing a little song and dance for the crowds, we got back in the car to go to town. Firstly, we called into Renaud's work for a snack, most of the staff couldn`t believe Norman was there. Some were from Albania and Norman's a bit of a god there. We got a good photo with all the staff. We then paid a swift visit to Doris who was working at a school for adults with learning difficulties. We didn`t really go in but Norman did go through the door and asked for Doris. When she arrived he gave her a big kiss and then we left. That was a personal favor to me, as Doris had been such a good friend I wanted her to feel special just for a minute. It made her day.

We went back to my house for a hour or so, Norman was keen to put one of his films on so we did. My neighbours come round again with their grandchildren, but most importantly for me, Mathew was there. Lisa was a friend that lived around the corner, Matt is her son who is a massive Wisdom fan. He had spoke with Norman on the phone one day at my house but he had never met him. We arranged with Lisa for her and Matt to come round. He wasn`t expecting to meet Norman and the shock on his face when Norman stood up to shake his hand was priceless. He wasn`t at all shy, he sat down and had a full conversation with SNW about his films and his career. Matt is one of the most intelligent, polite young men I have ever met and it was great to make his dream come true. I took Norman back just after teatime, my kids came with us for the drive. I gave Kim the money we had raised and thanked Norman for a smashing day.

A few weeks later he was back in Leamington again but this time it was his special day. I soon found ways to make these days good for Norman and one way of pleasing him was to call into a garage and look at cars. I rang the `Gaydon Motor Museum` near to where I live and asked them if we could take Norman around the cars for an afternoon. They said yes but they also said we could go for the whole afternoon including a party of guests for free, if we would allow them to take a photo. Obviously we agreed. I told Kim about the surprise, she said he would love it and we arranged a day. In the morning I was taking him to my college for a haircut, also cleared with Kim. I picked Norman up as usual, we drove up the M25 and the M40. Just as we got towards Oxford, Norman said he wanted a break and I needed the break too so we called into the services. Norman went off to the loo and I followed. As we were washing our hands this guy spotted Norman, he came over.

"Hi there, I am a fan of your work. I find the films you make are very exciting, very gory", he said.

I looked at Norman, Norman looked at me.

The guy continued "Is the makeup difficult to wear? Sitting around with all that blood and gore around you."

Norman was getting into it then, "Oh there`s no make up, its all real", and with that I told the guy we had to leave.

We sat in the corner of the services, fairly good sunshine, we had a coffee and a chocolate chip muffin each. I lit up a cigarette.

I was casually smoking it when Norman said, "I used to smoke Steve, I gave up 15 years ago. Can I have one?"

"No Norman, you can't!" I told him, "I'm not being the front page of the newspapers for killing you off with a fag."

"Killing me off, I'm 92 Steve. Did you know that?" he said

"Yeah Norman I know your age" I answered.

He didn`t reply for a few minutes, he was just looking at the water fountain.

"When I'm gone, all this will still be here" he said quietly.

"Yes it will probably be here, but the chances are when I'm gone too, this lot will still be here. Come on, lets go" I said to him, wondering what`s going through his mind.

In the car he was talking about his films, he asked me if I had seen any. I told him I had seen them all a dozen times and that I'd watched them with him. He seemed surprised. We arrived at my house around 11.30am, my parents were there and mum was looking very smart. Even Pete had his best tucker on. I had recruited the help of Dave again, not his car this time but his body (I wish). As he is in the Army, I thought he would be an ideal candidate to follow Norman around. It sounds stupid I know but some fans are quite rude, they will grab him by the arm and pull him around. I was very aware of his age and didn't want anyone pulling him around. Dave agreed, he's a good mate and I knew he would do the job well.

After a coffee I took Norman, mum and Renaud up to the college. My boss wasn't around but my tutor Tammy was there, along with Marj and Sharn, the students were quite busy practicing on dummy heads. Norman had a big smile on his face when he realized he was in a room full of women. Tammy cut Norman's hair, in between a few staff and students all asking for autographs. I kept some of Norman's hair. Joking with him I told him we could make a new SNW from the DNA. Dawn had come into the office, she was a manager but she was more than that. I always found her to have the most beautiful smile. I was pleased she could have a photo with Norman and my mum. We said goodbye and were standing near the lift as the doors opened, my boss was there, Jenny. It was a bad photo due to the confined space but I managed a photo with her and SNW in the lift.

We met Dave on route and went straight over to the Motor Museum. The convoy was two cars, myself, Ren, Dave and my Mum and Pete. There was a reception of staff waiting for us, of course Norman had to sit in every car in the Museum. He really was in heaven. We were looking at the sports cars when I saw Norman's face light up, in front of us was the most beautiful Rolls Royce Phantom. The lady showing us around came over.

"Do you like it Norman?" she asked

"Oh yes, she's beautiful" he said. "Smashing isn't she Steve?"

I agreed with him, just as the lady said "She's just over half a million pounds, I bet you wish you could afford one."

Norman swung round to look at her "I could buy four of them tomorrow" he said, turning back to me and winking.

I have to say the Museum staff looked after us very well, including coffee and cake and in return they only took a few photos. Now I tell everyone to visit the place, it's a great day out. This time I got Norman back quite late, I apologized (it was becoming a habit) and it was gone 1am by the time I got home to bed. It was a good day though, very happy memories. As I lay in bed that night, my mind was going through the day's events. Who was that guy in the services? Who did he think Norman was? Dave did a good job protecting Norman, he looked the part and I was very grateful. Norman sent Dave a signed photo thanking him for what he did but Dave lost the photo, shame.

I have been very lucky driving SNW around, all from writing to him as a fan really. I did nothing to push myself forward, albeit I volunteered my services for a few jobs. I am very lucky that Norman and the Wisdom family trusted me, but I could see he was getting older, I could see he was losing some of his memory. I spoke with Norman a few times about his work, films and stars. My favorites being Hattie Jacques and Jerry Desmonde. I asked him in the car what it was like working with Hattie, he replied with a big warm smile and repeated the words 'Heavenly, heavenly'. When I spoke about Jerry he seemed sad, he told me that Jerry had committed suicide and that a certain actor at that time had been the cause of it, by not letting Jerry out of a contract. Apparently he was held to this contract but was offered a leading role in a film. The actor wouldn't hear of Jerry leaving and this brought about a depression, which eventually took its toll. This was way after the Wisdom films. It's a shame really, Jerry was brilliant, very tolerant in Norman's films. I suspect it wasn't easy for him working with a perfectionist like Norman, I know Norman thought the world of him and vice versa.

In Sickness And In Health...Definitely

You may have noticed I haven't mentioned my ailments for a while, they were still there but after over 100 transfusions I had finally found a happy medium. I had found a way of calming down my illness and coping with it, my MS was steady, the Crohns was under control and my blood levels were quite good. I will be slated for saying this but for me, smoking helped a lot. Instead of junk food I was having a cigarette and this put less pressure on my stomach. I recently told my old surgeon about my smoking helping my ailments. He said "If it works for you, it's good." I'm going to die at some stage, whether it be smoking or MS or the Crohns or something different, I have found a happy medium I'm content with.

Of course, now smoking is socially unacceptable which annoys me. We are becoming a race of sterilized human beings, everything is bad for us, everything we do is dangerous or contaminated. You can even buy sterilizing gels to clean our hands and we buy them, including me. My Grandparents didn't have any of these gels, they lived until ripe old ages. My granddad was stopped from smoking by the hospital at 89 years old, he died a year later.

We often said to him, "Do you miss it Granddad?"
He said "I could kill for one."
Surely if the damage is done then it's done. Stopping smoking at 89, it's not going to repair his lung damage that much surely. I have a friend who I shall not name, they tell me off for smoking now, even though I am considerate and don't smoke in the room or around them. Some 10 years ago I didn't smoke and my partner did, along with the said friend. I sat most nights watching TV with them smoking around me or in bars with them around me, even in the car. I had to breathe their smoke for years, well now it's pay back. This isn't about `education', we all know what it does to our lungs, along with alcohol and drugs but any one of us takes a thousand more risks every day. I think people should just relax a little and if it takes a fag to relax then so be it. Rant over.

Kim sent me an email. Norman's memory was getting worse and they were considering putting him into a retirement home, I was devastated. I thought this was terrible, to dump him in a home and what... forget about him? I rang her up. I couldn't say much because when all is said and done it was none of my business. She said he was staying at their house for a month and then she was going over to look after him for a few months, Ann was retiring. Whilst on the island she was going to look for a retirement home. She asked if I'd like to see him, I agreed to come down and take him out for the day.

I took D&D with me along with Renaud. I thought this might be the last time I would ever be able to do this so I made a day of it. We got to the house and Kim made us a coffee. She said Norman was coming down in a minute and sure enough he came strolling through.

"Hi Norman, how are you?" I said.

He looked at me, "Who are you?" he asked.

At that very second Kim said, "It's Steve, Normee. Don't you remember him? He's been driving you around for some time now."

He looked at me again, "I recognize your face" he said.

"Once seen, never forgotten Norman", I said.

After a drink we got in the car and drove to Brighton, the strangest thing happened. We were on the marina walking around the shops and Norman pointed to the floor. "Look, it's me" he said.

Sure enough there on the floor at his feet was a stone flag, bearing the name `Sir Norman Wisdom OBE`. There was a walk of fame and a series of flag stones bearing famous names, we hadn't noticed them at all but Norman noticed himself immediately. We took a few photos of him pointing to the flag stone, it seemed to cheer him up. Nearby there were a fire engine and the firemen were raising money with a bucket, some charity I assume. I took Norman over and they were thrilled to see him. He stood for photos, standing on the step of the engine and posing with the crew. Some passersby came over for autographs. Darran was quick thinking and he told them that if they wanted a photo with Norman then they would have to put a few quid in the bucket. They did and the firemen loved it, good one Darran.

We went to Harry Ramsden's fish and chip shop near the Pier. As we took our table I could see people looking over. After such an eventful morning I was hoping we could all have some food without Norman getting pestered but within minutes this old lady came over. Not one to refuse, Norman signed her napkin. We ordered drinks and food, Norman was looking out of the window. I turned to see if he was ok and he was licking the glass.

"Are you ok Norman?" I asked, a little startled at what I was seeing.

"Yeah Steve" he said, "Look at the arse on her!" and he pointed to a pretty blonde crossing the road. We all cracked up laughing.

Whilst we were eating the lovely chips some women came over, they were early 50's but giggling like school girls.

"Can we have your autograph Norman?" they asked.

Norman opened his mouth with a half eaten chip mashed up in his gob.

"Huh, what do you want?" he said.

I stepped in quickly, "Norman they want an autograph" I said to him.

"What shall I sign?" he said and then pulling out a pen and grabbing a big long chip, he signed across it. With a silly grin he passed it to the women, blowing them a kiss. I was about to grab a napkin and they walked off, pleased as punch. I looked at Daniel and he looked at me.

"I wonder what that will be worth in 50 years" I said to him.

We paid the bill, just as we were leaving the waitress who was also in her early 50's asked Norman for an autograph. As he went to sign she dropped the pen, she bent over to pick it up and I tried to help. Meanwhile Norman had grabbed a plastic fork and he proceeded to push the fork against her bum. I jumped to try and stop him as the waitress said "Oooh Norman" and started giggling. Norman signed for her, gave her a peck on the cheek and we left. Now if that had have been you or me we would have got our faces slapped but oh no, not Norman. People loved him and the attention and worst of all, he knows it. Bless him. We did the usual tour of Brighton, looking for this theatre Norman insists is there. If you remember we've been there before; I finally got him home for 8pm.

I was in town when Rita telephoned me, Collect it magazine was in the shops, 10th July 2006. I called into WHS and there it was, I was on the cover with SNW. I bought 5 copies and went to a nearby café to read it. Ann E had made a great job of the story, I was thrilled and relieved. I'm not sure what lens Rob had been using on the camera but I looked quite sexy, (I thought). I immediately sent a copy to Norman. I telephoned everyone who knew me to remind them to buy a copy, and I telephoned Kim. Having had a good relationship with the Wisdom family, I wanted them to read the magazine, to see I wasn't doing anything behind their back. I don't know if they bought a copy but I know they read Norman's copy.

My plans for Spain were still on track, we had to choose a date so we decided on the 22nd October 2006. T&G were still living out there and I had asked them to find us an apartment so that at least we had a base out there. Dixi, my dog, had been through the hell of numerous injections so I could get her a passport. She was also going to the tanning booths in town to bronze herself up a little. Ok, that was an exaggeration but i`m sure she knew what was going off and I reckon she was excited. The plans to put Norman into a home were also going off, I still thought it would make him old before his time but then he was 92.

One of the last driving jobs I did for him was to the chiropodist. Of all the exciting places I'd taken him, famous theatres and hotels, all the beautiful places we had visited and we finished up after years of fun in a chiropodist. Yet even this was fun. Ann was back to give Kim a break, she was keen to move back to her home town where she had a beautiful cottage. I picked them up from Epsom, we drove down the M3 to Ann`s cottage by the sea. After a swift drop off we went round the corner to Ann`s sister. Norman had been quite a handful all the way down, he didn`t seem happy and was proving difficult. Ann`s sister invited us in and we had coffee and some lovely cake, (it must run in the family). Norman couldn`t settle, he was swapping seats, he wouldn`t eat his cake or drink his coffee, he was impatient and wanted to go outside. Finally we got him in the car to go to the chiropodist. As we parked up, some fans had heard we were coming and they waited outside, Norman enjoyed the attention and signed a few autographs. We went inside the surgery and he was called straight through, Ann accompanied him. Maybe 15 minutes later they appeared, I picked up Norman's jacket to put it on him. Ann was paying the bill and she asked Norman to sign the cheque, he signed it and then he turned to me.

"£25 for 15 minutes, it's a fucking liberty Steve" he said.
I told him it was cheap but he wasn`t having it.
As we got outside there were some more fans there. I asked Norman if he wanted a coffee and he said yes so I told Ann we would be in the café next door, she joined us a minute later. The fans came into the café and sat next to us. Of course, Norman was enjoying their company and he started acting around like he usually does, he ended

up kissing the women, tongue in cheek for a photo and then we left to go back to Epsom. We were back in his flat and Norman was quite tired. In fact, we all were as he had played us all up most of the day. Norman asked for the TV to be put on, I asked him if he had enjoyed his day out.

He said "Why, where have we been?"

"We've been to the coast Norman and to the chiropodist. Don't you remember?"

He said he didn't remember. I was disturbed; we had only got back 30 minutes earlier.

When I left I told him I would see him soon, Ann had agreed to stay a few more months I think to monitor if she could still cope with Norman. I was glad, if anyone could look after and care for Norman, Ann could. I had arranged another day out with Norman, my final before Spain. It was quite emotional for me, the family had been very kind to me. Ann had been welcoming and here I was planning a trip, which would take me a few years to complete. I didn't know what the future held. Would I ever see him again? Would he be at his home or in a retirement home? Would he remember me or would I be a stranger?

He was staying with his children when I picked him up. We drove down to Brighton, it was a well established run for me and SNW. I knew where to park, where he would be able to walk and I had one more idea. I stopped the car on the seafront, opposite Dora Bryan's house.

I turned to Norman "Shall we go and have a coffee with Dora?"

"Dora who" Norman said.

"Dora Bryan, we've been here before, she was in your films" I replied.

"I don't know her. No let's just drive around" he said "I don't even know her."

I was shocked, he had always had such affection for her and now he'd forgotten her and I think he knew he had forgotten because there was a hint of sorrow in his voice. We drove across the seafront to the marina and down to Peacehaven, Norman was quiet all the way. He was looking at the sea and the trees, turning his head to look at houses and shops, it was very surreal.

Finally, he said "I need a piss."

I said "Ok we`ll call in to the marina, there`s a café there."

We sat on the promenade of the marina, our usual spot. I ordered coffee whilst he went to the loo.

He came back and said "These people were asking me things in there, something about my films." "You're an actor Norman, you made some films. Don`t you remember?" I said to him, holding his hand. "No, well I think I remember some. I used to have a boat like that" he said pointing to a big boat coming into the harbor. "My boat was bigger, it cost me a small fortune."

"Did you build it yourself?" I asked him, knowing full well he had designed his own boat some 30 years earlier.

"No, my son built it" he told me, "Look out there, look at the sky. It's smashing isn`t it? What`s your name?", he looked confused.

"I'm Steve. Don't you remember me Norman? I'm your friend, I am driving you around today."

"Of course I do" he said with a big smile.

I knew he had forgotten me.

We drove back to the house, there was only Kim in the house, she put the kettle on. I sat in the lounge and Norman was in his chair. After a few minutes of watching TV he fell asleep. I reached over and stroked the back of his hands, he opened his eyes and looked at me and then closed them again. I just kept stroking this old skin, I was looking at an old face. This old man had given me so many wonderful memories and here he was in his 90`s and fading away. I said goodbye for one last time and got in the car. From the house to Gatwick, I was choking up. Tears pouring down my face, I saw the empty seat next to me and just broke down, I had to pull over. It was pathetic, he wasn`t even dead. I think it was a mixture of emotions and not knowing what the future held for both of us. You have to understand that meeting Norman did change my life, I was going off the rails before I met him. I watched him, learnt from him and it changed me. I keep telling my kids that everyone gets an opportunity and if you miss it, it could well have been your only chance. No, I'm not saying I could act like SNW. I`m a bit of a comedian but compared to Norman, my humour is vulgar. I don`t think Norman ever got fed up of the fame and the attention. I suppose he could have craved it but fame isn`t for me. Yeah i`ve told you about my life but I think it`s been interesting, it was my chance and I took it.

On the 22nd October 2006 we were ready, I had bought a seven seat VW Sharan. It was old but I'd had everything checked out. My parents told me they had two suitcases and a few bags, they turned up with twice as much. Luckily we had bought a trailer and a roof box too. Tension was high, we were worried about the journey, the car and the Spanish police. We had heard all kinds of stories regarding the Spanish police, never the less we got started. Mum and Pete were in the back, Renaud and Dixi in the passenger seat, Dixi`s bed on the floor and I was driving. I had the extra long mirrors and for the first 100 miles, I was watching for the trailer to fall off or the roof box to blow away. We arrived early evening into Plymouth but it took us over 2 hours to find a hotel. We wanted a safe car park because everything we owned was in or on the vehicle. Next morning we had breakfast and drove steadily to the ferry port. We got in the queue with another 700 cars, vans and wagons, it started raining. It was terrible, the boat was delayed by 6 hours, our car was stuck and we were bored senseless. We went for a walk with Dixi to the town, that got us all wet and when Dixi refused to walk anymore we carried her back to the car. Then we read, played on the laptop, listened to music and finally at 9pm, we were told we could board. Then it took another hour before our queue moved towards the boat. We were on board and after eating a hot meal, we started to feel a little sick so Renaud and I went to bed. I was worried about Dixi because she was in kennels on the top floor but when I checked on her she was sleeping. I woke around 6am, checked on Dixi but she was still sleeping so I walked on deck and got a coffee. I sat looking through the window at this glorious sunshine and the coast of our new country.

It wasn`t long before Renaud and my parents joined me. The coast looked beautiful, we were looking forward to a new day. I checked on Dixi and took her on deck for an hour. I had terrible nightmares that someone would break into the kennels and throw her overboard. She was sniffing the air, I wondered what she was thinking. Most likely she was thinking `I need grass to shit on, not green painted metal`, bless her. We got off the ferry and followed everyone else. We had our SatNav but most English cars were going the same way so we followed. It was quite sad really because every twenty miles we saw broken down English cars, we wondered if we`d be next but we kept plodding on. Luckily the SatNav took us around Madrid rather than through it, it was the middle of the night and we were doing a steady 50 mph. I remember this part quite well because Mum and Pete had dropped off to sleep, Renaud was dosing and I was driving a decent speed in comparison to the weight I was carrying and pulling. I knew if we broke down now, at least we were halfway and T&G would be available for help but the car kept going and so did I. In the middle of nowhere I pulled over for a 30 minute kip, I couldn`t sleep properly but it was a break. I drove a little more then we drove through mountains and down the other side, this time stopping for a good break and a coffee. There was a little shop open so we took the opportunity to practice some Spanish, luckily the bloke spoke English.

As we were sitting there at probably around 7am, there was glorious sunshine and we were looking at the hills we had driven over and at the vast fields of olive trees. I joked with my mum that she`d soon be working in those fields and we`d be able to see a cloud of smoke, knowing it was mum working. We all had a good laugh. I decided to text T&G to tell them where we were, I think they were surprised how far we had come. Dixi had walked around a bit, she was 17yrs old and my little girl. She seemed happy, urinating on anything resembling grass. We continued the last quarter, after maybe a hour or so I started recognizing areas which I'd seen whilst on holiday. It was amazing to see the signs for Malaga and then Churrianna, where T&G lived. They met us at the end of their street and we followed them to the apartment in Benalmadena. We had made it. I had driven the length of Spain and we were all fine, Thank God. It was a challenge to do this drive. Some people have probably done more, some less, but for me I was proud. I've had a few challenges in my life, some I've taken advantage of, some I've dealt with and I'm sure there's more to come. Whatever happens, I'll be doing my best.

Short of Time

This was to be the end of my book but as I said from the beginning, I've written it four times. Each time I've worried about getting things right and trying not to upset anyone. I've used no artistic license in my book, I've told no lies and the majority of dates or information has come from my letters. I'm a great collector and save everything I've received through the post or by email. This is mostly to remind me of dates for this book but I also wanted to cover my back.

I was travelling in Spain for 4 months before I flew back for a few days. Kim had sent me a few emails including an invitation to see Norman at his new retirement home. I was still worried about him and took up the offer. I flew to the UK, collected a hire car and drove to Liverpool with Darran and Daniel, we arrived on the Isle Of Man early morning. I drove over to Ballalaugh, Ann was there on her own. She looked lost and I could see she had been crying. I asked how Norman was and she said he's confused. He had been there only a week and he was constantly asking where Ann was and why he was there. The staff told him he was on a cruise ship and he seemed to accept that. I dropped Darran and Daniel off in Douglas and went with Ann to see Norman. I walked into the home quite stern, I don't know why but I was expecting an argument. Instead I thought it was quite nice. We were taken upstairs to a room and the door opened. On a chair in the corner of the room was Norman, he was asleep. We sat down next to him and one of the staff woke him gently, his eyes opened.

"Hello" I said, eagerly trying to gauge any sort of reaction.
His eyes lit up, "Hello Ann. Hello Steve, are we going for a drive?"
"Maybe later" I said.
I could see Ann was choked up, it was upsetting for her. I asked Norman what his cruise ship was like. "It's nice here Norman isn't it?" I said.
He looked over, "Yeah its nice, the grub is good and the women!!"
We all had a laugh. The staff took Norman down for lunch, we left also. I told Norman I would be back later and he said he was looking forward to it. Ann drove back to Ballalaugh whilst I went to meet Darran and Daniel.

Later that day we went back over to see Ann, she had a friend with her `E`, I didn`t know her but I could smell her feet, she was a real cow girl. They both seemed a little patronizing, I could see they had been drinking. The empty bottle in the kitchen and the half bottle in the lounge gave it away. I asked Ann about the family and this `E` butted into the conversation. She tried to tell us she had chosen the retirement home with Kim, I wasn`t particularly listening so I went into the kitchen following Ann. She was still a bit off with me so I asked her what was wrong. She blurted out a few things about the family and then she said something I'll never forget. "Nobody loves Norman like me, that family didn't see him from year to year. Do you know what I'm going to do Steve? I'm going to write my book!"

She had tears in her eyes, she was hurt. I went back into the lounge and Daniel and Darran looked pissed off, I could feel some tension so I suggested we leave. Ann gave me some of Norman`s things, model cars, his shoes and various bits so I put them in the car. Whilst I was in the kitchen, D&D were talking to `E`, she was being quite rude to them.
Out of the blue, she asked Daniel "Have you been educated?"
Daniel said "Yeah, I went to University"
Apparently that shut her up.

We were due on the ferry in 2 hours but I had promised Norman I'd call in to see him so we headed that way. I went into the reception and introduced myself. As I did, I saw Norman sat on a chair reading the paper. I was asked for a password, I gave it to them (Kim had told me it) and I went to sit with him. He was pleased to see me and we chatted about this 'beautiful hotel' he was staying at, the staff brought us both a coffee and a piece of cake. Darran and Daniel came to the door to say we had to leave, they had been waiting in the car. Norman saw them and as I was talking to them he came over and shook their hands. At that moment the staff came over and asked them for the password. They had no idea, I hadn't told them. I explained they were with me but the staff were having none of it so they were asked to leave. I told them I'd be down in 5 minutes.

We went up to Norman`s room and I took some chocolate out of my bag. I told him he was my hero and he asked why. I tried to explain but he was sleepy. I held his hand stroking the back for a minute, then I left whilst he was sleeping. We just about made it to the ferry port, we were one of the last cars to board. Whilst on board I telephoned Kim to tell her about the visit, she asked me what I thought of the home and I told her it was nice. I was lying but I didn't want to upset her. I did tell her the home was clean and the staff are really nice. I also told her what Ann had said to me and what `E` had said to Darran and Daniel. I should have been there, if she'd have said it in front of me I would have snapped, maybe it's lucky I wasn't. Anyway I thanked Kim and told her I'd be in touch. A few days later it was in the papers that Norman had been put into a home and it was dirty with plastic furniture and a hospital bed, like a institute rather than a home.

A few months later I asked Kim if I could go again, the family agreed so I booked my tickets. This time I was flying. I flew from Malaga to Manchester, stayed in a hotel and early morning I flew to the Isle Of Man. I jumped in a taxi to the home, when I arrived they were expecting me. I was given a towel (it was raining heavy) and then shown up to Norman's room, he was asleep. I sat there watching TV until he woke up. He was pleased to see me.

"Hi Norman, it's Steve. Do you remember me? I was here a few weeks ago with Ann" I said

"Oh yeah Steve, I remember" and he stood up to shake my hand.

We chatted for a while, this time the staff brought up a tray of cakes and coffee. They certainly knew the way to both our hearts. I left the Collect It magazine with Norman whilst I went down stairs for a fag. While I was outside I was talking to the staff. They were pleased as punch to be looking after Norman, they loved him to bits and being the older end they knew him from his films and like me, grew up with him.

When I went upstairs, Norman was looking a bit sheepish.

I asked him "What's wrong? What have you done Norman?" with a slight grin on my face.

He passed me the magazine and I instantly saw he'd written all over it

"Don't read it now, put it into your bag" he said, "read it later."

So I did. The staff told him it was lunchtime and they invited me to join them. I sat in the dining room and had a lovely meat pie and mash, just like my school dinners, I enjoyed it. Norman had a little bit but he was full with cake. We sat chatting to the staff and residents for an hour until Norman asked if we could go upstairs. I pressed the button for the lift and Norman said "No Steve, I'll race you."With that he set off running upstairs. I went after him but he was gone and waiting for me at the top.

We got to his room and decided to put a film on, `On The Beat` starring Norman Wisdom.

We were about 30 minutes into the film, when Norman said to me "What's this we're watching?"

I said "It's a film Norman, we chose it, why?" I asked

"Who`s that little man there? I don't think much of him" he said.

"It`s you Norman you plonker," I said laughing.

He fell asleep and I'm not surprised after the cake and the dinner I was feeling dopey, my eyes were closing slowly. I must have been gone five minutes when one of the staff walked in. "Hi there, oh is he asleep? I've brought some cake, biscuits and tea", she said. I was left alone again; I was looking at the picture on the wall, a good sized portrait of SNW and pictures on his window sill of Patrick, Ann and the family including grandchildren. There were books, DVDs, a flat screen TV and a stereo. Behind me were the toilet and shower room, a wardrobe and two sets of drawers. Norman was sat on his favourite big red chair from his house. The bed was in the corner and on the floor was a big rug from his lounge. He was fine, it was home in his mind. He was clean, looked well and was gaining weight. The staff are friendly, respectful and they adored Norman. What more can any person ask for? He had a full audience whenever he wanted it, there was a piano, a beautiful plush carpet and the cakes were to die for. I may have lied when I first spoke to Kim a month or so earlier but now I could see what they could see. I left whilst he was sleeping, I left a little early as the weather was bad and I was scared they would cancel my flight. I thanked the staff and took my taxi to the airport.

The weather was getting worse, I enquired about any delays and they told me numerous people had cancelled their flight. There were only 5 of us and we may be delayed by 20 minutes or so. We were delayed by an hour. I was glad to be called through, the plane was empty and the steward looked bored. I sat near the window as the plane took off, it was jerking and banging in the air. We were being thrown left and right, I was shitting myself. I took my mind off things by looking at the photos from my visit. SNW looked well in them, I did too actually. I wondered `again` if I would ever see him again and then I thought, it doesn`t matter because I'm going to die on this plane anyway. I was glad to land and get off. The journey back to Malaga was easier, I just slept most of the way and when we landed Renaud was there to meet me. Previous to the flight I had telephoned Kim to say how I had enjoyed the visit and how good the staff are with SNW and myself. This time I was telling the truth, I really felt he was in the best place.

I was telling Renaud and the words from Ann came into my mind, I kind of understand what she was saying. It is probably true that the Wisdom's only saw him once a year; he was working constantly, here and abroad. It took me ten years to meet them. Ann probably did love him like no other, she worked and lived with him 24 hours a day for years and she knew him inside out. I think everyone had an argument for their case but I came to the conclusion that if it was my dad, I would want the best. From what I could see, he has it. I told Kim this by email, everything about Ann, the home and my recent visits. She told me it was difficult for them, everyone had their own agenda and theirs was to care for SNW as best as possible. I was sure they had done the right thing and the shit they had to put up with was wrong. It was their business and their father.

I've had a few visits since the last two, some from Spain and more recently from the UK. Yes, we are all back and glad to be. The adventure was good but there's no place like home. It's a good job we came back, I caught a disease in my eye and 2 years on I'm still fighting it. I now wear glasses. Within months of being back, my mum discovered she had breast cancer. She had the operation last year to remove two lumps and touch wood, she`ll be fine. As for Norman, well he's settled in his retirement home. We recently had an invitation to visit him again, this time Renaud came with me as he hadn't been on the island before. In July 2009 we flew to the Isle Of Man, hired a car and booked into a sea front hotel. We were meeting the Wisdom family at the home around 11.30am.

We drove up and waited for them, this time the weather was lovely. When they arrived we were taken into the home, the doors had new security locks. This was due to the amount of press and fans that kept trying to walk in and interview Norman. We went upstairs and he was in the same room. He was awake for a change and genuinely pleased to see us, I presented him with a framed picture of us both, the photo is my favourite. It was taken by Kim whilst on one of my day`s out with Norman. He looked at the picture and then me and then back again. I told him when it was taken and by whom, he accepted my gift and put the picture on the windowsill. It was difficult to talk to him like I usually do because everyone was there around us. Renaud was watching TV and the family were just looking at me. Norman was quite cheery, he was talking about the weather. I was reminding him of our days to the seaside and Dora`s. He didn't remember but it didn't matter because I could repeat all my stories and he'd listen to them like it was the first time he had heard them. Of course in his head, it was.

After maybe 30 minutes, we left promising to be back the day after, he said he was looking forward to it. We said goodbye in the car park, me and Renaud wanted to explore some of the island so we decided to look around Douglas first. After a bit of shopping we went back to the hotel for something to eat. I had a message on my phone from Kim inviting us for a glass of wine at Ballalaugh, Norman's house. It was up for sale and they were staying there, sorting out the things they wanted to keep and selling the bigger items they needed to get rid of. After a brief kip, we set off around the island via the Laxey Wheel, Ramsey and Andreas a beautiful village near to Ballalaugh.

I kept saying to Renaud "You'll know the house when you see it, it's beautiful."
I was driving down a lane when Renaud said "Look at that one, that's nice."
As I looked left I braked hard, "That's it, that's Norman's", the brass plaque on the wall confirmed it.
We had a lovely evening with Nick and Kim and their boys. We chatted for hours about Norman and me, they learnt a lot about our relationship and I learnt a lot from them. I felt we had finally got to

know each other, finally they understood me and I them. When we left that night I said to Renaud "I think that evening was a long time coming, I think we have made some good friends".

The next day we went into Peel, a seaside port I often went to with SNW when I was visiting. I think this was the time Renaud actually fell in love with the Isle Of Man, I could see he thought it was beautiful and he said so, often. We had a look in a few antique shops, in one of them I bought my dad a lovely handmade silver ring with a tiger's eye stone. On the left of the jewellers was a bookstand so I had a look through the books and on the bottom shelf was an autobiography of a famous British comedian. His name was Sir Norman Wisdom. I bought the book for £8, it was his first ever autobiography. I had seen it but never read it before, I opened the front cover to find it was a first edition. We bought some cakes from the bakers and set off to meet the Wisdom's at the retirement home. I was thrilled with my purchase and couldn't wait to show them.

As we arrived at the home Nick and Kim arrived, this time the kids were with them and we went upstairs to see Norman. He was in a jovial mood, he had remembered me which was a nice surprise and he was obviously thrilled to see his grandchildren. We sat there for 30 minutes chatting and taking a few photos when I suddenly remembered the book. I started to tell them about it when Kim asked where it was. I had left it in the car so me and Nick went to fetch it. I showed it to Kim, pointing out the 1st edition inside.

She said "Ask Norman to sign it."

I hesitated which is unlike me, "Maybe next time" I replied.

She looked at me, "Steve, there may never be a next time", she was right.

I took the book over to Norman and asked him, "Norman will you sign this book for me?"

"Yeah Steve" he said and he took it from my hands.

He always liked to have a quick look at these things before he signed it them.

He had a flick through it and then asked me, "Who to?"

"To me Norman!" I said with a laugh.

The book is `Cos I'm a fool`, 1996 First Edition and he wrote inside, `With best wishes Steve, Sir Norman Wisdom.'

The Show Must Go On

I hope you've enjoyed the book, I enjoyed the memories. The week I finished this book was the first week of January 2010. I've got a bad back, probably from sleeping on my mum`s couch over the New Year. There's a couple of things you might want an answer to. The `Collect it` Magazine SNW signed whilst I was visiting him; you may remember he wrote on it and told me to put it in my bag to read it later. Well, he had written `With best wishes to you Steve, from your good old pal, Sir Norman Wisdom OBE. And with best wishes finding yourself a smashing bird, in fact a really gorgeous tart with a couple of big and gorgeous tits, that would be lovely so make the best of it Steve.`

I thought this statement was great, its Norman's humour. He knew I was `gay` but to him it meant nothing. This is the humour I loved from Norman, I love him to bits and I treasure the magazine.

I said early in the book that something happened, something changed my life recently, well it was a tattoo. I have a full abdominal scar, it saved my life but the scar bothered me. Recently whilst Renaud was in France I went to see a tattooist, friend of mine called James. I asked him if he could tattoo over a scar, he said yes if it was quite old. I went through agonizing pain whilst he tattooed my stomach, when he was colouring over the scar I thought I was going to faint. When he had finished, I was shaking from head to foot, I told him I was cold. When I got home I had a coffee and a fag and watched TV for an hour. I had a long hot bath that night and stood in the mirror looking at the new art work. I have rarely been so proud, I had no scar, I had a design. Thanks James, you have no idea how you changed my life.

Oliverboi@Hotmail.com

Sir Norman Wisdom died on the 4th October 2010'

Norman Wisdom O.B.E.

To Dear Steve.

Thanks for all the driving, and it was nice being with you. Wishing you good luck for the future for your new life in Spain.

With best wishes for

Sir Titch Wisdom.

Miss Norman.

4/2/15 - 4/10/10

To my brother Jason, your a Hero to this family and we love you x

Lightning Source UK Ltd.
Milton Keynes UK
171757UK00002B/8/P